NIGHT OF THE TOXIC SLIME

The slime edged forward towards the road that lay between marsh and sea. The tide was out and muddy sand stretched towards the line of distant lapping waves that glinted in the early light of the June morning.

Slowly, relentlessly, it began to slide across the road, long, thin and bubbling, about half a metre wide. There was a hissing sound and the surface began to melt, the acrid stench of hot tar blending with the vomit-making smell of sulphur.

A creeping fear seized Jake – a fear of the unknown that he had not experienced in years.

Point Horror has mutated…

MUTANT
Point Horror

NIGHT OF THE T☢XIC
SLIME

Anthony
Masters

SCHOLASTIC

Scholastic Children's Books,
Commonwealth House, 1–19 New Oxford Street,
London WC1A 1NU, UK
a division of Scholastic Ltd
London ~ New York ~ Toronto ~ Sydney ~ Auckland
Mexico City ~ New Delhi ~ Hong Kong

First published in the UK by Scholastic Ltd, 2000

Copyright © Anthony Masters, 2000

ISBN 0 439 99640 6

Typeset by TW Typesetting, Midsomer Norton, Somerset
Printed by Cox & Wyman Ltd, Reading, Berks.

10 9 8 7 6 5 4 3 2 1

1

Jake skidded his bike to a halt, choking and gazing down at the filthy stuff in revulsion. A long finger of slime was sliding across the rough marsh grass, dribbling in fits and starts, pushing itself forward jerkily. What the hell was it, he wondered. Untreated sewage?

The grey-green slime was oozing under the wire fence that surrounded the Craven Marsh Ministry of Defence research station. It was making a slight bubbling sound and had the sulphurous smell of rotten eggs.

The slime edged forward towards the road that lay between marsh and sea. The tide was out and muddy sand stretched towards the line of distant lapping waves that glinted in the early light of the

June morning. The weather had been hot for weeks and the heat was already oppressive. The time was just after six on a Saturday, and there was no traffic.

Just as well, thought Jake, as the slime began to climb the grassy rise to the road. What was propelling the stuff? How was it dribbling uphill? Then Jake started as he smelt scorched grass and saw the slime was leaving a burnt and acidic-looking trail.

Slowly, relentlessly, it began to slide across the road, long, thin and bubbling, about half a metre wide. There was a hissing sound and the surface began to melt, the acrid stench of hot tar blending with the vomit-making smell of sulphur.

A creeping fear seized Jake – a fear of the unknown that he had not experienced in years.

The research station had been on Craven Marsh for as long as Jake could remember. Long, single-storey, prefabricated buildings were laid out in an H block, with worn dry grass in the centre, enclosed by a heavy-gauge mesh fence with razor wire at the top. Faded signs all carried the same message: MOD PROPERTY. DO NOT ENTER.

At the front of the compound, just off the road, were two large, locked, rusty iron gates, also with razor wire on top, and a security barrier just behind them.

Like everyone else in the area, Jake had no idea

what went on inside the research station, and because the place was a familiar sight that he passed every day on his way to sixth form college, he had forgotten to be interested.

Years ago, local rumour had ranged from talk of chemical experiments to animal vivisection and from secret missile manufacture to a new kind of GM crop. But now the place had a deserted, abandoned look, and although there were a few cars in the compound during the week nothing much seemed to be going on.

To Jake, and in particular to his close friend Laura, the place was an eyesore; Laura's family, ardent environmentalists, had been running a local campaign for years, attempting to force the MOD to close the research station and have Craven Marsh returned to the public.

A wind was coming off the sea, blowing Jake's untidy blond hair into his eyes. He was tall and well-built and had always been good at sport. A mountain-bike enthusiast, he liked to get up early and put in some training. As soon as college closed for the summer he had planned to ride out here every morning.

A year ago, Jake had been popular and sociable, but ever since Mum had left Dad to live in Folkestone with a bloke she'd met, he'd lost his confidence. He no longer played for the college football and cricket teams, devoting himself to his beloved mountain biking instead, which also gave him the freedom to get away from the cottage when Dad was in a bad mood, cycling hard across the flat marshes, exhausting himself.

The only person he was really close to now was Laura. At first she'd been sympathetic and supportive, but lately Jake felt she was finding him a bit of a bore.

Unlike Jake, Laura seemed to have plenty of confidence and they often quarrelled. But he was determined that Laura wouldn't always get the upper hand.

"You're self-obsessed," she had told him during their last big row.

"And you're trying to eat me alive," Jake had yelled back at her.

"I thought there was a nasty taste in my mouth," she had replied.

Jake shivered in the cool, early-morning air. The slime was halfway across the road now, pulsating like a snake with indigestion, making a sizzling sound.

Suddenly a piece oozed out from the main section, rather like the tentacle of an octopus, heading his way, spluttering at him. Jake's revulsion turned to apprehension again. What was going on? Was the wind blowing the stuff at him? But it wasn't that strong…

As the tentacle came nearer, the smell of sulphur intensified, the vile stench getting up Jake's nose and down into his lungs, making him gasp for breath. His feet felt rooted to the spot. It was as if the slime had him under some kind of hypnotic spell.

Somehow, using a huge effort of will, Jake broke out of his trance, turned and began to pedal back in the direction from which he'd just come. But he'd only covered a few metres when he braked hard and skidded round in a circle.

Mesmerized, he watched the tentacle withdraw into the main body of the slime, the tarmac continuing to sizzle as the stuff headed for the beach.

"*You!*"

The voice made him jump so badly that Jake felt a renewed rush of panic. He got off his bike and stood staring ahead, focusing on the distant sea which looked as if it was frozen in time, a picture-book ocean, unmoving, flat and soundless.

"*You!*"

Jake turned awkwardly and sound and movement seemed to abruptly return again. A bizarre figure was standing by the rusty iron gates of the research station, clad in protective clothing and talking rapidly into a mobile phone. He was holding something in his other hand that was now pointing at Jake. The thing was snub-nosed. Surely it couldn't be a gun?

Again panic swept Jake. Was he caught up in some kind of emergency?

The man put the phone back in his pocket and gazed at him thoughtfully.

"Raise your hands and start walking towards me slowly."

Jake was shattered. Nothing ever happened in these parts. You had to create anything out of the ordinary for yourself. Now it was being created for him.

"I repeat, raise your hands and start walking towards me slowly."

Feeling both absurdly melodramatic and increasingly afraid, Jake put his hands above his head and began to walk towards the man in the protective suit. As he did so, the slime made a rustling, rattling sound as it started to ooze over the pebbles on the beach-head.

"Stop there. What's your name?"

"Jake Oakley."

"Address?"

He began to shake, hardly able to speak without stuttering. "Four, Hill Rise Cottages, Shingleton." Suppose the man shot him? Suppose he was going to be compelled to wipe him out because Jake had seen something he shouldn't?

"What are you doing here?"

"I'm in training for a mountain-bike rally."

"Early, isn't it?"

"I'm an early riser."

"Get your bike and clear off." The man gradually lowered the gun so that it hung by his side.

There was a short silence during which Jake was surprised to feel a strong sense of anticlimax. "What is this stuff?"

"Chemical leak. Now – clear off."

"What is it? Some kind of acid?"

"On your bike."

Jake began to walk back and then paused. The slime had come to a quivering halt on the pebbles, but a scorched trail still stretched across the road.

"Do I ride over that stuff?"

"Go back the other way." The man's voice was expressionless.

"It's miles round."

The man ignored him. He had dragged out his mobile phone again and was muttering into it, glancing at the road and then back at the slime.

Jake had almost reached his bike when he heard the sizzling. Turning back, he saw the tentacle heading towards him again, much faster than before.

"Run!" shouted the man in the protective suit. Now the fear was in *his* voice and he seemed more afraid than menacing.

As Jake ran, he glanced over his shoulder to see the tentacle speeding up even more, the acidic trail scorching the tarmac again.

His heart hammering, Jake ran faster, but he

could hear the sizzling sound getting louder and nearer. Leaping over his mountain bike he ran on and then turned to see the tentacle of slime had reached his bike and was trailing over the brightly-coloured paintwork.

The sizzling became a burning and Jake's new, beautiful, multi-geared mountain bike with all its much-prized accessories began to melt in a cloud of steam. He gazed back, not believing his eyes. This couldn't be happening. But it was.

Rage began to overcome his disbelief. The mountain bike had been his most prized possession, his means of escape. Now it was molten metal – metal that was fusing with the burnt and melted tarmac.

The man in the protective suit was back on his mobile.

"Look at my bike!" Jake yelled, anger masking his fear.

The man jammed the mobile back in his pocket. "You shouldn't have stopped."

"That slime stuff came after me."

"You shouldn't have stopped," he repeated in a monotone.

"How was I to know? What are you going to do about my bike?"

"Someone will be in touch." The words hung in the sizzling air like a threat.

Jake stared down at what had once been his new mountain bike. Now it was a puddle of liquid metal from which the tentacle was gradually withdrawing.

"You'll have to pay for this!" he yelled.

"Someone will be in touch," the man repeated doggedly, watching the tentacle with what Jake sensed was the same disbelief he himself had experienced.

The tentacle returned to the main body of the slime which was fast retreating under the wire of the compound with a spluttering, hissing sound. Soon it had disappeared, and all Jake could see was a burnt trail through the grass outside the wire, runnels in the tarmac where the surface had melted away and the pool of liquid metal which was all that was left of his precious bike.

"Clear off," said the man in the protective clothing. "Now!"

An electric humming filled the air and Jake started, his heart hammering again, beads of sweat breaking out on his forehead while the man with the gun swung round to check the perimeter fence of the compound.

Instinctively, Jake began to stumble across the marsh towards his home town of Shingleton. The road was completely clear now, but he couldn't bring himself to tread on the spot where the slime had been. Suddenly, raw terror had him in its grip, and his sweat turned cold, making him feel as if he was wrapped in a thin sheet of ice.

What was the foul-smelling stuff that had eaten

the grass and the tarmac and, eventually, his bike? Could it have consumed him? And why had the security man been dressed in a protective suit? Why had he got a gun?

Gasping, Jake paused and looked back, only to see that the electric humming was coming from a milk float that was bumping over the ridges burnt in the road.

There was the sound of a siren, and in the far distance Jake could suddenly see a shimmering mass of vehicles on the road through the marsh, almost as if they were a mirage.

Then the image of the convoy became sharper and Jake could see jeeps, armoured personnel carriers and, finally, a Jaguar with blacked-out windows travelling towards the research station at speed. All the vehicles seemed to be sounding sirens now, all were flashing lights.

As the milk float drew over to the side of the road, the convoy thundered past while, out of the dawn sky, came the chattering sound of a helicopter.

The sun slowly came up.

Jake was fit, but the shock was destroying the rhythm of his breathing and he soon had to take a break. Panting and glancing back yet again he could see the long convoy had drawn up beside the research station. Barriers were being erected a little further down the road.

The milk float was rattling back the way it had come and a few vehicles were also turning round and doing the same. After a while the road emptied completely and Jake guessed more barriers had been erected further up the marsh.

Running on, his heart pounding, Jake began to fear pursuit. He imagined figures crouched behind bushes, parting the foliage, watching him menacingly. Then he thought he saw someone streaking after him, but it was only a shadow caused by a cloud passing over the sun.

Trying to take a grip on himself he increased his speed, but skidded to a dead halt when he thought he saw something move on the ground in front of him, softly slithering like a snake. Then Jake realized that what he was staring at so fearfully was only a broken reed from one of the ditches that ran across the marsh.

Glancing back for what seemed the hundredth time, Jake saw the Jaguar with the blacked-out windows begin to glide away from the research station, heading slowly in the direction of Shingleton.

He wondered uneasily where it was going as he stumbled over the tussocky grass, his legs feeling like lead, his head aching badly, still mourning the loss of his beloved bike. What had he seen? A chemical spill with a mind of its own that could shoot out a tentacle and reduce a bike to molten metal? How *could* that have happened? Jake began to feel confused, not able to remember exactly what had happened and in what order.

He slowed down again, giving himself a much-needed break, hands on knees, bent double, then straightening up to watch the stationary convoy. The army vehicles must have come from Folkestone Barracks so whatever had happened must have been classified as a major incident. And why did the Jaguar have blacked-out windows?

Jake turned away and ran on, less worried about pursuit now, another concern taking over. Just what was Dad going to say when he told him about his bike? He was bound to go ballistic. As a fisherman he only just scratched a living and Jake knew how hard his father had worked to save up for the bike.

Then he remembered the words of the man in the protective suit. *Someone will be in touch*. The phrase began to beat in his head. *Someone will be in touch. Someone will be…*

Jake had been born in Shingleton and had always loved the town with its steep streets, rising above the working harbour where the fishing boats were anchored.

He had never grown tired of the place, despite the fact he was sure Laura thought him un-adventurous. But even she had enjoyed going to sea in the *Lucky Strike* with Dad and Uncle Ben.

Jake and Laura had met at the sixth form college in Folkestone. Laura wanted to be a journalist, but Jake had decided to work for his father and uncle who were about to buy another small trawler. Jake loved the sea too much to think about doing anything else.

As he puffed up the steep hill to the cottage,

Jake thought about his absent mother, which he did every day. She ran a hairdressing salon. The tension had been bad at home for a long time, but he had been as surprised as Dad when she'd told them she was leaving. Of course, he saw her every week and he even quite liked Bill, her new partner, who owned a garage and had grown-up kids of his own. But the fact that she had gone was like ice in his heart.

Turning the corner, Jake came to a sudden halt, his mouth dry and a leaden feeling in his stomach. Parked outside the family cottage was the Jaguar with the blacked-out windows.

Someone will be in touch, the man in the protective suit had said. *Someone will be in touch.*

As Jake passed the driver's open window he could see a chauffeur sitting behind the wheel, dressed in a black peaked cap and dark suit, doing a crossword puzzle.

Jake knocked on the front door of the cottage apprehensively, forgetting he had a set of keys.

"What's got into you?" said Dad. His weathered face was deeply tanned and his long hair fell on his shoulders in ringlets. Jake, who loved him dearly, often thought he looked like a pirate. Mum had always been urging Dad to get a haircut and "smarten up". She was a bossy sort of woman – a bit like Laura.

"Who's in there with you?"

"Lost your keys as well as your bike?" But Dad didn't look bad-tempered – which he often could be. He just seemed puzzled.

"I've got my keys."

"Why not use them then?"

"Are you going to tell me who's in there with you or not?" Jake was out of breath and exhausted. His temper was rising, but so was his anxiety.

"Bloke called Millard."

"Who's he?"

"Head of Security at Craven Marsh."

"What does he want?"

"You'd better come in and find out."

Millard was slightly built with a neat military moustache, swept-back dark hair, an old school tie, blazer and dark trousers.

He got up and shook Jake's hand briskly, his grip surprisingly strong. "Sorry about what happened. Must have shaken you up a bit. We've never had a leak before so we had to call out a full scale alert. Of course the media are going to pick up on it, but I do hope you're not going to talk to them."

"Don't get you," said Jake, who wanted to sound surly. He didn't like Millard. He was too glib.

"It means I'm going to ask you to be discreet."

"Why?" Jake wasn't normally this aggressive; although he had a temper it usually burned on a long fuse. Now he felt that the fuse had been burning for a long time.

"Because our work at Craven is secret."

"What *is* your work at Craven?" demanded Jake. He was still shocked and confused, and was wondering what on earth this dapper little man was going to do about his melted-down mountain bike.

"He's just told you – it's secret," rapped out Dad.

"Well, I can assure you we're not all mad scientists. I'm going to confide in you both," said Millard smoothly. "As much as I can, anyway. After all, we're conducting experiments that are very beneficial to the environment – but we don't want commercial interests getting in on the act. Hence the discretion. They'll only over-charge and we want our substance to benefit the taxpayer. Eventually."

"Substance. Is that what you call it?" Jake was still aggressive and his father frowned. "Do you realize what just happened?"

Millard held up a protesting hand. "The fact is that our experiments are directed at producing a substance that will destroy household and industrial waste and eliminate the use of landfill." He spoke as if he was reading from a prepared script. "What I'm trying to get across is this: there's a great deal of protest coming from environmentalists – and not *just* environmentalists – about filling up the countryside with the kind of rubbish we can't recycle. With our new chemical we hope to be able to destroy even metals within seconds. I'm only sorry that the leak took place."

"There was this security guy in a protective suit. He had a gun." Jake was determined not to give in to all this propaganda.

"The chemical is very toxic," explained Millard with a patient smile, "so the formula has the highest security profile. You saw what happened to your bike." He laughed heartily. "I'm sure you wouldn't want that to happen to you." Was there a hint of a threat in his voice?

"So that slime is a chemical – a highly toxic chemical?"

"It is indeed." Millard's grin seemed to stretch his whole face.

"Isn't it dangerous to have the stuff sliding about?"

The grin was frozen. "We don't have it sliding about. We have the chemical substance safely stored in underground tanks."

"You didn't this morning."

"That's why I'm here to apologize. We had a faulty valve – hence the leak. It won't happen again."

"That's what they say about nuclear accidents," said Jake belligerently. "Yet it doesn't seem to stop them."

"This has nothing to do with a nuclear accident," said Millard firmly.

17

"But the slime can melt stuff."

"Not if it's contained." Millard's smile now looked as if it had been engraved on his face.

"Jake," interrupted his father, "you're being very difficult about this."

"What about my bike?"

"That's another reason why I'm here," said Millard and handed Jake a cheque.

When he looked down, Jake saw to his amazement that the cheque was made out for £1,500.

"That's far more than you paid for the bike, Dad," he said, his aggression temporarily forgotten.

"That's what I mean. Mr Millard is being very generous."

But is he buying me off, thought Jake.

"I realize that you'll have some money over," said Millard, looking more relaxed. "But, after all, you had a very nasty shock and you deserve a little compensation."

"That stuff's lethal." Jake returned to the attack.

"We'll make very sure it's safely contained in future. We've never had a leak before and we don't intend to have one again. I'm only sorry you were the innocent victim." Millard's voice was brisk and less sympathetic now.

"He can't say fairer than that, Jake," said Dad.

"No," he mumbled, deciding not to push things any further.

"Get yourself a new bike, with all the accessories you need. And, by the way—" Millard hesitated.

"Yes?"

"If you *are* contacted by the media, I'd very much appreciate you *not* talking to them. We need to reduce waste-tipping and stop infilling." Once again Millard sounded as if he was reading from his script. "This has to be the way ahead. What we don't want is private enterprise moving in. And no media reports about Frankenstein's Laboratory, either." Millard gave another of his hearty laughs.

"I see what you mean," said Dad. "We don't want the gutter press poking about on the marsh."

Jake groaned inside. Dad was always on about the gutter press. It was his favourite subject.

"I must be going," said Millard, shaking hands with Dad and Jake.

"Well – thank you again," said Dan Oakley. "I'm sure Jake is the lucky one. We appreciate your visit – and your gift."

"Just compensation for your loss," said Millard as he opened the front door. "The last thing we all want is the tabloids snooping about on the marsh and interfering with such a beneficial scientific experiment."

As Jake and his father stood on the doorstep watching the Jaguar drive away, Dad said, "I must say he's been very generous."

But Jake knew that Millard hadn't been generous at all. He had just been trying to shut him up.

He suddenly felt deeply ashamed and decided to ring Laura as soon as he could. Jake had no intention of being paid off just like that.

3

Jake knew his father would be bound to try and overhear what he was going to say to Laura, so he made an excuse and hurried down to a telephone at the bottom of the road. It was ten o'clock and there was hardly anyone around on the Saturday streets.

Dialling Laura's number, Jake felt nervous and defensive, for he knew he should never have accepted the cheque and had played into Millard's hands. But what would he do without a bike? Especially a mountain bike?

Laura had been increasingly impatient with him lately and Jake had been partly angry at her treatment and partly apprehensive. He knew she didn't think much of fishing as a career. Well, let her go to that tinpot university, Jake thought. He didn't need a degree to be a fisherman.

But then, of course, there was Chris.

Jake barely allowed himself to think about him.

Of course Laura wasn't going out with Chris; he was just part of the group she hung around with, that was all. Clever, intelligent, good-looking and sporty, Chris was going to the same university as Laura. How Jake hated the bastard.

"Yes?" Her voice was crisp.

"It's Jake."

"Oh, hi. Look, I'm just going up to the squash club for some coaching."

"Something's happened."

The tone of his voice brought her up short and Jake was pleased.

"At home?" she asked anxiously.

"I was out on my bike and I saw this stuff."

"What stuff?"

"Kind of slime. Right across the road. It ate my new bike."

"It *what*?" She was completely thrown.

"I told you."

There was a pause and then she laughed. "OK – so slime ate your bike. That's nothing new. You hardly ever cleaned the last one. Look, Jake, I haven't got time for this. The squash coaching's very expensive and if I miss—"

"So was my bike. Now it's just a puddle of

molten metal."

"What?"

"My bike was expensive," Jake explained patiently. "The slime ate it away – like the stuff was made of acid."

"The bike?"

"The slime, you prat! I'm not joking. It happened outside the research station," Jake continued doggedly, wondering how long it would take to convince her.

"Craven Marsh?"

"Where else?" Jake began to explain what had happened and Laura was suddenly and un-characteristically silent.

"You could have been eaten away yourself."

She was really convinced now and Jake began to take pleasure in her sympathy. Then he made the mistake of mentioning the cheque.

"You shouldn't have accepted it," Laura snapped immediately, no longer worried about the threat to his life. "You've taken a bribe."

Jake felt a flash of temper, knowing he might have expected this from Laura. He was already kicking himself for taking the cheque and she had rubbed his nose in it.

"Am I going to see you today?" he asked.

"I've got to work on my history project this afternoon. But I could meet you down at the Fox at seven. If you like." She sounded unenthusiastic.

"I would like," snapped Jake. "But I hope you're not going to spend the evening patronizing me."

"Now why should I do that?" asked Laura.

Jake decided to take a walk up the beach that afternoon. *Lucky Strike*, the Oakley family trawler, was having some repairs made to her hull and wouldn't be able to put to sea until tomorrow.

He felt exhausted by his early rise and what had happened, but Jake's curiosity had got the better of his fatigue. Although the long walk over the pebbles was punishing he would eventually arrive opposite the research station. Jake wanted to see what was going on and if the convoy was still there.

His father had been as difficult as Laura over lunch, still angry over his rudeness to Millard, but Jake knew that the shock of his mother's departure had caused lasting repercussions for both of them.

"OK," Dan Oakley had repeated, "so you had a bit of a fright. But there was no reason to speak to the man like that. He was only doing his job."

"I had more than 'a bit of a fright', Dad." Jake had been indignant. "If that stuff ate my bike, then it could have eaten me."

"Come on—" his father had begun.

"You ought to have seen the bike," Jake had snapped, but had given up the argument before there had been a row. Once Dad got obsessed with something he wouldn't see anyone else's point of view.

Jake climbed up the ridge of pebbles to see what was happening. There wasn't a car in sight, but these days most people took the new dual carriageway that ran inland rather than the winding sea road, however beautiful the view.

He almost ducked down as he saw an open truck with a couple of men loading traffic cones and barriers, but they didn't even glance at him. Jake knew he had every right to be there, but he decided to keep to the beach.

He soon came alongside Craven Marsh research station and once again clambered up the ridge.

The cluster of huts and long, low prefabs were as silent and deserted-looking as ever, separated by strips of ragged, marshy-looking grass and tarmac that was scarred and dotted with weeds. There was no one around and the wire surrounding the compound sagged. What a dump, thought Jake. Then he wondered if the research station was deliberately left to look a mess so that no one would reckon the place had any importance.

Jake, however, was becoming increasingly convinced that the slime was of the highest importance.

He slid back down the ridge to think, but was suddenly overcome by a grinding fatigue. He lay down, wedged himself into the pebbles behind a breakwater and fell fast asleep in the early afternoon sun.

The slime was coiled around Jake's body in thin, pulsating strands while the acid began to eat into his flesh. He watched his hands melt until only skeletal fingers were left.

Jake woke to a choking scream which at first he thought might have been his own. Sitting up, he glanced around in the afternoon heat, for a moment not sure where he was. Had he really screamed, or was it someone else? The tide had gone out and there was a smell of brine – and something else that was familiar, but which he couldn't immediately identify. Then the scream rang out again and this time he was sure it had come from behind the breakwater.

He got to his feet. Acres of flat, wet sand stretched

down to the edge of the sea. Then he recognized the smell. It was sulphur.

Jake saw a thick finger of slime streaming out from behind the breakwater to form a smoking runnel in the sand.

He ran at the knotted, seaweed-hung wood, shinning up on top and staring down.

Below was a boy he vaguely knew from college – short, stocky and dark-haired. With him was a girl he had never seen before. She was tall, willowy and blonde, but her face was contorted with fear.

The slime glittered in the sunlight, looking more toxic than ever.

Then Jake saw smoke rising from the pebbles. "What's going on?"

The boy he now recognized as Tod Martin was streaking up the beach, but the girl was stock-still as she screamed and screamed again.

The tentacle of slime came slithering and smoking over the pebbles, a long, thin strand moving fast. Dropping her bag, she ran at the steep side of the breakwater, trying to climb but finding difficulty in getting a foothold. The tentacle lashed out in pursuit as she scrabbled, whimpering with fear.

Jake grabbed the girl's arm to pull her up just as the tentacle began to follow, melting the bag as it went, eating into the wood, scorching through the seaweed.

The girl looked up at Jake, her mouth opening and shutting but no sound coming out.

"What's your name?" shouted Jake, trying to get through her paralysis.

"Dawn," she whispered.

"Get a move on, Dawn. While you still can."

The tentacle was only half a metre below her now, reaching for Dawn's foot as she began to climb, hauled by Jake. Then she slipped and hung in space, legs flailing.

"I've still got you," he yelled.

Dawn edged up a little and he pulled harder. Jake had developed a very strong grip from years of working on the trawler, and now he yanked at her wrist so hard that Dawn cried out in pain. He dragged her over the top of the breakwater and then fell backwards, both of them ending up in a heap on the pebbles.

Dragging himself to his feet, Jake climbed back up the breakwater and watched the tentacle retreat into the thick finger of slime which hissed back up the beach and across the road with incredible speed.

Was the stuff reacting to some kind of recall?

The slime left a steamy, smoking trail.

Tod Martin picked up a pebble, suddenly dropping it with a howl of pain. "This is red-hot," he said, gazing down in disbelief.

They stood on the ridge, staring at Craven Marsh

and the MOD research station. Except for the scorched tarmac and burnt trail of grass there was no sign of the slime. But they could still smell sulphur and there was an acidic haze.

"It's gone back under the fence," said Jake. "Just like this morning."

"You seen that stuff before?" demanded Tod.

"It melted my bike – and would have melted me. There was a security alert and the road got closed off."

"No one told us," he complained.

"They wouldn't. It's a secret."

Dawn was thanking him for his help, but Jake barely heard her. He felt completely incredulous. What the hell was going on? How had another leak occurred so soon after the first?

"What's this secret then?" asked Tod, shaking. "It's not right." He put his arm around Dawn protectively, but she shrugged it off.

"It's some kind of experiment – a substance that apparently melts down household waste. This makes two leaks in one day, so they're really getting careless."

"I want compensation," said Dawn. "That thing melted my bag."

"Dawn's right. We need compensation." Tod was flustered and guilty at deserting her. "It's not just the bag. She could have got melted too. She could have ended up in a right state."

"OK," snapped Dawn. "No need to go on."

"Let's go over the road and check the place out," said Jake, trying not to think what Dawn would look like in total meltdown. It didn't really bear thinking about.

There was no sign of a bell on the outside of the Craven Marsh compound.

"Oi!" yelled Tod. "Anyone at home?"

In the eerie silence, a light evening breeze stirred the rank grass that struggled up through the tarmac.

"Where do they keep this slime stuff, then?" Tod persisted. "How did it get out?"

Jake shrugged. "Underground storage tanks, apparently," he muttered.

"It was only an old bag," said Dawn, unnerved by the silence and the desolate buildings. "Let's go back."

Tod gave her an impatient look. "Don't you want compensation?"

"I want out," Dawn replied bleakly.

"Where do you live?" asked Jake, hoping they'd go. He wanted to be alone. He wanted to think.

"Davington," said Tod. "We walked down to the beach for a quiet – you know –"

Dawn turned to Jake. "You saved my life. If it hadn't been for you, I'd be dead. And Tod didn't do much to help, did he?"

"What did you expect me to do?" Tod snapped. "Take on that stuff single-handed?"

"You let it attack me," she complained. "If it hadn't been for this guy—"

"I've got to be getting back now." Jake glanced down at his watch. He had to meet Laura at the pub in an hour and he didn't want to be late. He had a lot to tell her. "I should get away from here – like fast."

Now the tide was out he decided to jog back along the sand. Tod and Dawn were quarrelling fiercely now and they hardly noticed him go.

"I could have ended up a stain on the pebbles for all you care," she shouted.

"What did you expect me to do about it?" Tod bellowed back. "Wrestle the stuff to the ground?"

"It was on the ground already, you coward," Dawn retorted.

Their voices mercifully faded as Jake increased his speed over the hard, wet sand.

The pub was noisy and crowded and at first Jake

couldn't spot Laura at all. Then he saw her at a corner table. But she wasn't alone. Chris was with her.

Jake swore under his breath, and then tried to look cool and laid-back as he pushed through the crowd towards them.

"Jake." Laura seemed almost too attentive, as if she was trying to cover something up. "I'm sorry you had such a rotten time this morning."

"I've had another rotten time this afternoon," Jake said shortly. He dragged across a spare chair and began to explain what had happened.

Chris watched him intently, no doubt wondering if he was exaggerating. Tanned and good-looking, he always seemed confident and completely at ease. Chris had curly black hair, broad shoulders, chunky features and played rugby. He was popular with everyone – except Jake.

So what was he doing here, Jake wondered. And more importantly, how long had he and Laura been sitting together?

When he'd had finished there was a long silence. Chris glanced at Laura.

"This is getting ridiculous," she said. "Two leaks in a day. That stuff sounds lethal."

"Didn't you try to alert anyone in the compound?" Chris sounded disapproving. Was he hinting Jake had mishandled the situation?

"I told you – there was no way of alerting anyone."

"They just ignored you." Laura was scoffing. "They don't want to answer a lot of awkward questions, that's all. Someone needs to *do* something."

Jake and Chris were silent.

"We need to get into that compound," Laura continued.

"We?" Jake was badly shaken and even Chris looked uneasy. "We can't possibly do that."

"Why not?" demanded Laura.

"We'd be done for trespassing," said Jake, feeling flat *and* negative.

"So you're going to wait until someone dies?" said Laura brusquely.

"How do you plan to get in? Just shin over the wire? Or shall I buy some wire-cutters?" he asked sarcastically, convinced she was only winding him up. Winding them both up.

"That's not a bad idea," said Chris, seizing the initiative.

Laura turned to him eagerly. "Have you got any?"

"What?"

"Wire-cutters. What do you think I meant? A JCB?"

"No," he replied hurriedly, and Jake could sense Chris thinking fast. "But I can easily get some. My uncle's got this salvage company."

"Cool," said Laura.

Now Jake felt even more the outsider. Laura and

Chris seemed to have got it all sewn up between them and unless he wanted to be marginalized he knew he had to grab some of the action.

"We're only going to get away with this if we go in as protestors. Otherwise we could just be seen as yobs or vandals." Jake could still hardly believe they were all talking like this. Had Laura taken leave of her senses? OK, she believed in direct action, but wasn't this a bit over the top? Or even totally over the top? After all, Laura was calmly suggesting breaking into a top secret government department, wasn't she?

Chris seemed dismayed, as if he wished he had made the point. Seeing that he had Laura's attention, Jake hurried on.

"We should be able to fuel the Craven Marsh campaign if we find out what this slime is."

"Above all," put in Chris hurriedly, "we need to find out why and how the stuff keeps getting out. Even if the chemical *does* dispose of waste, it has to be controllable. So far the only casualties are a mountain bike and a bag, but what happens if the slime touches a human being?"

"It could be you," said Jake. "Or any of us," he added hurriedly. "All those emergency vehicles didn't show up for nothing." He paused. "I've checked out the TV news on Ceefax and there was nothing mentioned. So the MOD seem to have some clout."

"Of course they've got clout. They can do

anything they like – however dangerous, however anti-social." Laura was back on her soap box, but Jake was sure Chris was as alarmed as he was. What was she pushing them into? They could all get into real trouble for this.

Laura's eyes fixed on Jake. "And they'll have even more muscle if they know they can bribe people."

"I lost a mountain bike," snapped Jake.

"You lost more than that," she replied cuttingly.

Jake walked home feeling completely humiliated. The night was hot and sticky with the odd growl of thunder in the distance. The decision had been taken to break into the compound tomorrow night and he was desperately worried, cursing himself for foolishly trying to get one up on Chris, for backing a stupid plan that could only end in disaster.

He was eighteen, for God's sake, and was behaving like a jealous seven-year-old. What he should have done was to put a spoke in the scheme, bring them down to earth, stop them both being so damned stupid. But he hadn't. Laura had even devised a plan to fool their parents. She wanted them to make out they were all going to sleep over at Chris's house to revise for the exams. Chris, on the other hand, had been instructed to tell his parents he was going to sleep over at Laura's.

Jake supposed that Laura and Chris's parents

would accept the situation, but knew that his own father wouldn't be such a walkover.

But when he got home, Dad surprised him by being understanding for a change. "It helps to test each other out before an exam. I reckon that's a good idea."

Little did Dad know what kind of testing out they had in mind.

Jake went to bed and lay awake for a long time, listening to the growling thunder slowly dying away. All he could think of was Chris and Laura sitting together in the pub, and it wasn't for a long while that he fell into troubled and restless sleep.

"You lost more than that," Laura's voice repeated over and over again in his head.

Next morning, Jake overslept and found a note by his bedside. RISE AND SHINE. GET SOME BREAKFAST FAST, AND MEET US DOWN AT THE HARBOUR.

Jake was furious. Why couldn't Dad have woken him?

When he finally reached the quayside he found that the *Lucky Strike*, with a newly painted hull and decks gleaming with varnish, had been launched off the slipway and moored up to the side.

Ben Oakley was on deck while Dad was below, checking the engine. Ben was a few years younger than Jake's father and Jake always enjoyed his uncle's company. He had worked on oil tankers for years and had been round the world a couple of times doing some kind of scientific research that he never discussed.

Ben had never married and was tall and lean and permanently tanned, with a shaven head and tattoos all over his arms and chest.

When he had finished his research last year, Ben had proposed going into partnership with Jake's father, but Dan had been anxious. "Ben's always been a main-chancer. He'll have to keep his aggression – *and* the booze – under control if he wants to work with me." But because his original partner was always off sick and was also incredibly lazy, Dan had taken Ben on and together they had bought a much more modern trawler, which they named *Lucky Strike*.

For his part, Jake had been delighted by the arrival of his uncle. Ben made him feel free, in charge of his own destiny, admiring him for wanting to make a life as a fisherman. Lately, his uncle had done a good deal to boost Jake's confidence and for that he would always be grateful.

Ben was also a hard worker and had soon won Dan over. "I've got to hand it to him," Dad had told Jake on several occasions. "Ben's really got stuck in. I take back what I said about the guy. He's boosted our income and given you a future. So mind you don't forget that."

Jake hadn't.

The morning was cloudless, the air fresher, and

the picturesque stone-walled harbour at Shingleton was looking at its best. The fishing fleet was small but had been making money out of a fisherman's collective that had been formed a few years ago. A lot of work had been put into the collective by Ben.

Now a new shed had been built on the quayside to sell fresh fish, there was a boiling house for whelks and another new building that processed shellfish. Ben had clearly been an enormous advantage to Shingleton with all his energy and commitment.

Even now, he was polishing the brass rails and getting the *Lucky Strike* shipshape before she set out.

On the way back from the fishing grounds, Ben was usually at the helm of the trawler while Jake and Dan gutted the fish – a messy but complicated job. But on the way out Jake was at the wheel, mulling over the events of yesterday and worrying about tonight.

As Ben came into the wheelhouse, he glanced at Jake and said, "You look knackered."

"Thanks."

"Exams burning you up then?"

"They're a lot of hard work." Jake gazed ahead, keeping on the compass bearing, knowing that if he made a single slip he'd get severely criticized by his father.

"How's that mouthy girlfriend of yours?"

"Being mouthy," said Jake sourly.

Ben grinned. "I hear you had a bit of trouble yesterday morning."

"Only lost my brand new mountain bike."

"And had it replaced with a little bit more on the side." Ben winked at him.

"I got a cheque for £1,500."

"Generous."

"That guy, Millard, was just trying to shut me up, I guess. I should have chucked the cheque right back at him."

"And gone without a mountain bike?"

Jake said nothing, staring ahead, checking the compass, screwing up his eyes against the sun. The sea was calm and there was very little wind.

"I don't know what to think," muttered Jake.

"I bet your lady friend does."

"What's that supposed to mean?"

"Has she been telling you what's what about that cheque?"

"I don't get you."

Ben looked impatient. "She been telling you that you should have given Millard his cheque back?"

"She might have done." Jake was surprised by Ben's perception.

"You don't like that, do you?"

"I told you – I don't know what to think."

"Well, in my opinion it was a generous thing to do. Millard can't buy your silence. You can still give him a hard time."

"There's something weird about those leaks."

"I thought there was only one."

"I mean – leak. Why? Have there been others?" Jake hadn't told his father about yesterday afternoon and didn't want Ben to latch on to it.

"Not to my knowledge."

"I don't like the place."

"If they're trying to help the environment—" began Ben. "Think of all that rubbish littering the planet."

"Maybe you're right," said Jake. "But it's the method that worries me."

"The method?" Ben looked puzzled.

"That slime stuff. It's lethal."

"It would have to be pretty toxic to do its job."

"Then why isn't the stuff kept under control?"

"There's obviously an investigation going on into that."

"They seem to want to keep it very hush-hush."

"Once the tabloids get in on the act every cowboy could get involved. As you say, it's dangerous. Surely there won't be any more spills – not after what's happened."

Ben seemed to be as paranoid about the tabloids as Dad, Jake thought in disappointment.

"She's the boss then, is she?"

"Eh?"

"Laura."

"Why should she be?" Jake was immediately on the defensive.

"I know when you're feeling down, Jake. It *is* Laura, isn't it?"

"So what?"

"You need to think more of yourself. Why don't you bring her out in the boat?"

"We went out a couple of weeks ago."

"Liked it, did she?"

"You know she did."

"You're a son of the sea, Jake. You're not university material."

"Suppose I wanted to be?"

"You've got a great future here. The fishing's doing well and we've got the quayside up and running. With an extra boat we can do pair fishing in the winter. All we need is another hand, and I'm keeping my ear to the ground." He laughed. "Unless Laura fancies having a go. Why can't you persuade her to give up on university and get real?" Ben clapped Jake on the shoulder and went out on deck again.

7

Once the *Lucky Strike* was a couple of miles offshore the winch dropped the nets into the sparkling, still-calm ocean, while the sun beat down.

Jake went below to make sandwiches and brew up tea which they ate and drank on deck in companionable silence.

For a while he fantasized about Laura joining as a deck hand, imagining them both working together in unlikely harmony on a brand new trawler which, naturally, Jake skippered. Laura obeyed his every command, openly admiring his expertise. "Aye, aye, sir," she said dutifully, saluting and letting him show her how to gut a pile of cod. "Am I learning fast?" she asked him. "Will I ever be as good as you?"

Jake smiled at the unlikely conversation and drifted off into a slight doze, his back against the wheelhouse, the tea in his mug gradually slopping on to the deck.

He was woken by a friendly kick from Ben. "We're going to winch the nets in," he said. "If you've got a moment, that is."

"What's the matter with you, son?" asked Dad. "Why can't you keep awake?"

Ben winked as Jake struggled to his feet.

The nets seemed unnaturally heavy.

"Hang on a sec," said Ben and Jake slowed the winch. "We don't want to do any damage."

They gazed into the bottom of the net. There were quite a few fish, a large number of crabs scuttling about – and a length of grey-green material.

"Slime," Jake muttered to himself incredulously.

"What?" Ben's voice was sharp.

Jake didn't say any more as his father swore. "What is it?"

"Pipe-weed," said Ben. "Either that or plankton. It's polluted, of course. The stuff's turning up all over the Thames estuary."

"I don't think so."

Jake knew he had to speak up, but could hardly get the words out. Suddenly the sunlight was chilly and the sea looked malevolent. A seagull alighted on the rail and made a bleak rasping sound.

"That's a piece of toxic slime," Jake said quietly.

"What are you on about?" snapped his father.

"The stuff that leaked out of Craven Marsh. A bit of slime must have got into the sea – and we've picked it up."

"Nonsense." Ben sounded impatient. "That's polluted plankton, that is. Lower the nets and we'll get rid of it."

"Then we'll lose the whole catch," complained Dan.

"Better than losing the net."

But as they dithered Jake could see they were already too late.

There was a hissing, sizzling sound, the familiar smell of sulphur and part of the net began to melt.

"Sod the stuff," yelled Dan. "Drop the net."

Jake worked the winch as hard as he could, wondering if Ben was right. He *hoped* he was right. Before, Jake had only seen liquid fingers of slime. This was a lump and there was no sign of a tentacle. Yet the colour was exactly the same. As he lowered the net back into the water as fast as he could, the hissing, sizzling increased in volume.

Then, with what was left of the net trailing back into the waves, it burst, spilling the catch and floating, torn and ragged, on the surface.

Dan and Ben swore. "That's definitely polluted plankton," said Ben. "I've seen it before."

"Plankton that burns through nets?" asked Jake.

"There've been other cases."

"What cases?"

"Cases I've heard about—" Ben's voice tailed off, as if he had lost confidence in what he was saying. Then he became even more forceful. "I know what I'm talking about," he snapped.

Jake felt a sudden burst of rage. Why didn't anyone ever take him seriously? He wasn't a kid any longer.

They all three watched the torn net drifting on the swell with something moving in its layers.

"Your plankton's got a life of its own," sneered Jake.

"It's just the tide moving the stuff about," Ben insisted.

"Sure."

"Of course it's plankton." Dan Oakley had clearly decided he was going for the rational explanation. "Chemically polluted plankton. Wasn't George Benson talking about it in the pub?"

Ben said nothing.

As Jake walked towards the beach he knew he had been dreading meeting Laura and Chris at Craven Marsh, but now he also felt a sense of relief. The last two days' chilling events were weighing on his mind to such an extent that he desperately needed some kind of resolution.

The leak that had destroyed his bike, the leak that

had destroyed Dawn's bag, the piece of slime in the net – so far only material objects had been damaged. But that seemed to have been just a lucky coincidence. He could have died, Dawn could have died, Dad and Ben could have died. It had to stop. Jake had to find out how to make it stop.

After they had moored the *Lucky Strike* there had been unfamiliar tension between him and Ben and Dad.

Ben had tried to ease things by giving him one of his mock punches that actually hurt and saying, "I don't want to argue with you, Jake. I know you had a nasty experience yesterday."

Jake decided to meet his uncle more than halfway. "I'm sure you're right about the plankton. But where do you think it came from?"

"They say the pollution's brought in by the tide from hundreds of miles away." Ben had been vague and hadn't said who "they" were.

Jake had nodded and his father had said, "I don't care where the bloody stuff's coming from. All I care about is the state of my net."

Later, Dan had called up another skipper on the trawler's radio and Jake had listened in.

"Hello, Tango Four. This is Tango Twelve. Over."

"Tango Four. I'm receiving you, Dan."

"Just lost my net to that polluted plankton. You heard about it?"

"Not a lot. Didn't George Benson have a bit of trouble last week? Hole in the net, he said."

"The stuff's just chewed through mine. It's got to be reported."

"George's done that."

"So what's happening?"

"Coastguard's been having a look."

"And?"

"Hasn't come up with anything yet."

"Fat lot of good that is."

After a few more complaints his father had wound up the call, absolutely certain now that Ben had been right.

Jake felt a new determination to find out what was going on, however great the risk. So they had to break into a top secret security area. There was no choice. Not any more.

The research station looked even more desolate and abandoned in the moonlight.

Laura and Chris both looked nervous but purposeful, and Chris had brought some wire-cutters – but only two. Of course, thought Jake. Did he really work at putting him down, or was it all instinct?

"Don't I get a pair?" he asked.

"That's all I could get," said Chris shortly.

"Let's go round the back."

They trod carefully over the boggy ground, and although Laura had brought torches none of them dared use them. The night was still and quiet, and all they could hear was the sighing of the waves and their own plodding footsteps.

Once they arrived, Jake could see the wire was looser here and bulged badly. He squatted down and checked. "All we have to do is cut it here and we can squeeze through." Jake gazed through the wire at the compound, but there wasn't a light shining or the slightest hint of human occupation. "Listen," he whispered. "We picked up something weird in the nets today."

"Weird?" asked Chris.

"My uncle said it was polluted plankton, but I'm sure the stuff was slime."

"Why?" demanded Laura.

"It burnt a hole in the net and smelt like sulphur."

"You're sure you weren't mistaken?" demanded Chris belligerently. "Like mistaken all along?"

There was a long silence.

"Ask Tod and his girlfriend. After all, they've seen the slime too. It went for Dawn." Jake paused and then hissed at Chris aggressively, "You think I'm lying, don't you?"

"No," said Laura firmly.

"Let's go for it," said Jake, grabbing a pair of the wire-cutters. He felt powerful, almost invincible.

8

As they crawled through the wire, Jake had a sudden and rather obvious thought. If the slime was so top secret, why was it so easy to get into the compound? It was almost as if a trap had been sprung.

As soon as Jake was through and clear, he lay on the grass, listening to a slight humming which sounded like some kind of refrigeration unit.

The moonlight was strong enough to pick out a number of circular discs in the ragged grass, each with a kind of valve at the top.

As the other two lay on their stomachs beside him, Jake whispered, "They must be the underground storage tanks. Can you hear that humming sound? I think it's getting louder."

"What are you expecting?" asked Chris. "Frankenstein's Monster?"

"Or the Slime Creature from the Black Lagoon?" Laura's feeble joke died on its feet.

"Neither," said Jake. "I'm looking for something much more lethal. I've also got a feeling that the whole research station could be underground and anything on top is just a façade."

"That's all a bit James Bond, isn't it?" said Laura.

"Is it?" asked Chris unexpectedly. "To go underground would seem the most sensible thing to do if the MOD are manufacturing something top secret. But since when did the Ministry of Defence get tied up with household waste? It's not their job, is it?"

"It might be," said Laura. "Waste is a real threat now."

"But suppose the slime doesn't have anything to do with waste," Jake whispered. "Why should we believe that smoothie Millard? The slime could be manufactured for an entirely different reason."

Laura froze. "What's that?"

A slopping sound rose above the humming.

"Suppose the slime's getting active again?" Jake hissed, real fear sweeping him for the first time. There was an urgency to the slopping that he didn't like. He passed the wire-cutters back to Chris and flashed his torch briefly around the compound. In its beam they could see a scorched trail leading from the discs towards the wire which had been partly burnt away.

"Isn't that enough evidence for you?" whispered Jake triumphantly.

"So what happens next?" said Chris, looking down at the circular tanks – if they were tanks – and their valves. The slopping sound was louder as if something was coming to the boil.

"Let's check out the buildings," said Jake, switching off the torch. "If there is some kind of underground complex there must be a way down."

They stood up, gazing around them.

Suddenly, as if an alarm had been triggered, the lights in one of the prefabricated buildings flashed on, and at the same time powerful spotlights bathed the compound in flat, white, stark light.

They stood there, feeling completely exposed, too terrified to move.

A door opened and there was the sound of frenzied barking. In the steely light a couple of Rottweilers padded out, hackles up, teeth bared, stopping just short of them.

Jake could hardly believe what was happening and his former confidence vanished.

"For God's sake!" whispered Chris. "What the hell are we going to do?"

"Don't move," said Laura. "Dogs like that are trained to kill."

"You're exaggerating," hissed Jake.

"Who says?"

"He's *hoping* you're exaggerating," whispered Chris.

A figure in a boiler suit approached, giving muttered instructions to the Rottweilers. They reluctantly crouched on the grass, eyes fixed on their victims.

"How did you get in?"

There was a long silence. Then Laura said in a monotone, "We cut the wire."

"You know this is MOD property?"

"Yes," said Jake.

"You've seen the warning notices—"

They nodded.

"So why are you committing a criminal act of trespass?"

"This is a protest," said Laura.

"A *what?*"

"A protest."

"What about?"

"The toxic slime."

"Come again?"

"The toxic slime," Laura repeated, giving Jake and Chris an accusing glance, obviously feeling she was being made to do all the work.

"I don't understand what you're talking about."

"She's talking about the toxic slime," said Jake.

The conversation seemed to be going round in circles.

"You lot seen too many sci-fi movies?"

"No," said Jake. "There have already been two leaks – and I've seen both. The first time round the stuff melted my bike and this guy Millard came to my house and—"

"So you're just a bunch of students," interrupted their interrogator dismissively.

"No way," said Jake.

"So what are you then?"

"We're concerned about the leaks," said Chris.

"So are we."

"What are you doing about them?"

"We had a defective valve. The fault's been corrected."

"There were two leaks." Jake was persistent. "What's going on?"

"The fault's been corrected. Now I'm going to have to detain you while we call the police. Breaking into a MOD security area is a very serious offence." He gave a muttered instruction to the Rottweilers who got up snarling and salivating. "Follow me, please."

As they reluctantly obeyed, Jake was sure that both the humming and slopping sounds were growing louder.

They were led into one of the derelict-looking buildings and then down an empty corridor which looked long disused, a couple of bare bulbs picking out damp stains and mould on the walls.

Their captor unlocked a door and showed them inside a small bare room with a battered plastic table and chairs standing on a threadbare carpet. There were bars on the small window and more damp stains on the walls.

"I'm afraid you'll have to wait here until the police come."

The Rottweilers were pacing up and down, growling.

"We'll simply tell them we were making a protest against those leaks," said Laura. "You should be prosecuted for polluting the environment and putting the public at risk."

"What's more," said Jake, "my dad picked up a piece of slime in the net of our trawler. The net got burnt away by the acid – and we lost our catch. So we need compensation from the MOD which is another reason we're here. The police should be interested in that." Jake was surprised at his fluency and he thought for a moment he saw a flicker of doubt in the man's eyes.

"There's nothing sinister here and the police know all about us. We're here for the benefit of the public."

"Why are all these buildings derelict?" demanded Laura. "Where do you work?"

"I suggest you mind your own damn business. Haven't you caused enough trouble?" Then he spotted the bulge in Chris's jacket pocket. "Wait a minute – what have you got there?"

One of the dogs padded nearer and Chris hurriedly handed over the wire-cutters.

"Damaging MOD property. That'll be another charge." Calling to the dogs, he added, "I'm going to ring the police now."

He slammed and locked the door behind him, leaving the three of them alone in the musty little space.

Chris squatted down on the floor. "We'll get nicked for this – we could even do time." He suddenly seemed younger and more vulnerable.

"We're protestors. It's political," persisted Laura feebly.

"We'll get done for breaking and entering as well as trespassing and anything else they can throw at us. What about the exams? What about college? We could be expelled."

"Good to hear you being so positive, Chris," sneered Jake.

"Shut up and listen," whispered Laura.

Brisk footsteps were coming down the corridor. Then the key was abruptly turned in the lock.

"Mr Millard," said Jake nervously.

Millard looked shaken. "Jake Oakley — what in God's name do you think you're playing at?"

He said nothing. No reply seemed adequate.

"And who are these two?"

Jake noticed that Millard's fists were clenched and there was a little pulse beating in his temple.

"I'm Laura Knights and this is Chris Cornford." She was trying to be defiant but only succeeded in sounding rather pathetic.

"Are you going to explain yourselves?"

"We're very concerned about what's going on here," said Jake, stumbling over his words. "I got involved in one slime leak—"

"And you were handsomely compensated," snapped Millard.

"And there was another a few hours later. But it didn't get the same kind of attention, did it? No alarms. No one in protective suits. No military convoy. Not even a gun in sight." Seeing Millard's discomfiture, Jake grew more confident. "Tod Martin, a student I know from college, was on the beach with his girlfriend when the second leak took place. The slime melted her bag – just like it melted my bike – and then one of the tentacles chased her up a breakwater. The stuff could have killed her – just like it could have killed me." Jake paused, noticing that Millard was glancing out of the window. "I should never have taken your bribe."

Millard swung round. "What bribe?"

"Your so-called compensation. You just wanted to shut me up, didn't you?"

"There's nothing to shut you up about," said Millard. "Except we didn't want you bleating to the press for the reasons I stated."

"We had to make a protest," said Chris doggedly. "It was in the public interest."

"You broke into an MOD security area." Millard made eye contact with Laura. "What we're doing is in the public interest. As I told Jake, we're developing a chemical substance which is designed to dramatically reduce household waste – a much-needed experiment to eliminate the use of landfill."

Jake noticed Millard was back to his script again. "Why should we believe you?" he demanded.

"Because I'm telling you the truth." Millard still kept glancing out of the window. The tension in the room was increasing and Jake had a strong feeling of something about to happen, of something running out of control.

"You're just a spokesman," said Laura witheringly.

"Someone's got to be. Look, I'm sorry. I was generous to Jake but I can't go on being generous. I'm going to call the police."

"That's what your colleague said."

"I wanted to talk to you first and make you aware of the seriousness of what you've done."

"You've had two leaks," said Jake. "Isn't what *you've* done serious? That stuff is lethal."

"The leaks won't happen again," said Millard crisply. "The faulty valve was hard to locate—"

"Then why do you keep looking out of the window?" asked Jake.

"How do I know there aren't more immature students wandering about out there? We don't want our commercial competitors to benefit from any stupidity on your part. They'll only rip off the public if the contract's put out to tender."

"Why's your security so poor?" demanded Chris. "That wire outside's sagging."

"That doesn't give you the right to cut it."

"Your research station is underground, isn't it?"

said Jake, seizing the opportunity. "That's why you don't give a sod about the perimeter fence. It's irrelevant, isn't it?"

"So are you going to ring the police?" asked Chris. Suddenly there was a hint of pleading in his voice.

Don't betray us, thought Jake. Don't even think of letting him know we're scared.

"I'm afraid I can't let you off," said Millard with a slight smile, and Jake cursed Chris again. "It's more than my job's worth. I've tried to be reasonable."

"What about our parents?" asked Chris, making it worse.

Wimp. The word blazoned across Jake's mind.

"The police will be in touch with them – I can assure you of that." Millard began to walk towards the door. "I'll arrange for some coffee and sand-wiches to be sent over. Never let it be said that Craven Marsh doesn't look after its intruders." He opened the door, closed and locked it without any further comment and they could hear his footsteps echoing in the corridor.

"Now what?" asked Chris.

"You didn't have to grease up to him," said Jake.

"Shut up!"

"Oh, shut up, the pair of you!" Laura intervened. "There's no point in us falling out. In fact, I got the impression Millard was as scared as we were. But he was scared of something different."

"What?" asked Chris.

"I'm sure he wasn't worried about other intruders," said Laura.

"Maybe something's gone wrong again," said Chris. "Maybe one of his monsters is breaking up a lab. Maybe Godzilla just got out."

Jake went to the window but the spotlights had been switched off.

After about half an hour, their original captor arrived with coffee and some rather dried-up looking sandwiches.

"Are the police here yet?" demanded Jake.

"They're coming." The man's hands shook slightly as he placed the tray on the desk.

Jake caught Laura's eye. She looked both curious and alarmed at the same time.

When he had gone, Jake tried to lighten their apprehension. "What have we got here? Slime sandwiches?"

Laura laughed. "It looks like an ancient form of spam, or is it just processed human flesh? Either way, I'm starving." She bit into one of the sandwiches. "It doesn't taste of anything at all."

"That's because it's been genetically modified," observed Chris gloomily.

An hour passed and there was still no sign of the police.

The room was hot and stuffy and Jake had the

impression it was getting smaller all the time. He kept pacing around and then staring out of the barred window into the darkness beyond. But nothing stirred.

Meanwhile, Chris and Laura sat on the floor and stared into space, which Jake found increasingly irritating.

"Quit pacing," said Laura, obviously finding him equally annoying.

Chris looked up at him balefully.

"I don't want to sit down."

"You're getting on my nerves," said Chris.

"Oh dear, I'm really sorry about that."

"So sit down and be civilized."

"Civilized? You look like a monkey in a cage. A wizened monkey, or maybe a baboon – one of those with a red arse."

"Don't be childish," snapped Laura.

"Maybe the police aren't interested," said Chris with sudden hope.

"Maybe they haven't been called," Jake suggested.

"Why do you say that?" asked Laura.

"Suppose Millard just wants to give us a scare? He could lock us up all night and release us tomorrow – just as a warning."

"That's not what he said." Laura looked puzzled. "He seemed determined to call them."

"Could he have changed his mind?" Chris was even more hopeful.

"I've had another thought," said Jake impatiently.

"Well?"

"Suppose Millard doesn't *want* the police around. Is that why he was looking so scared? There could be something here he doesn't want them to see."

"Like the slime?" suggested Laura.

Another hour went past. They were quieter, more united now, listening to the silence which seemed to deepen, to hold them suspended in time.

Jake had sat down beside them and slowly they began to doze. Then he woke to find Chris snoring loudly.

He nudged Laura.

"What is it?" she muttered blearily.

"Still no police."

"What's the time?"

"Coming up to four."

"What are we going to do?" She sounded dependent on him for once and Jake felt a rush of adrenalin.

"I'll go and bang at the door. I'm not putting up with this." He tried to sound more aggressive than he felt. "It's like we got abducted."

He scrambled to his feet and went over to the door, pounding on it and wrenching at the handle. But no one came.

"Let us out!" yelled Jake. "What's happened to the police?"

Chris woke with a start. "Who's that?" he yelled. "What's going on?"

"It's OK," said Laura shivering. "Jake's trying to get hold of someone. It's been hours and the police haven't turned up yet."

"Come on," bawled Jake, pounding at the door again. "What the hell are you doing? Where are the police?"

When he stopped banging, the blanketing silence returned, but just as he was about to pound at the door again, Chris whispered, "Hang on."

"What is it?" Jake whipped round, but now he could hear the faint sound for himself.

"It's that slopping noise again. But louder."

Jake went to the barred window and Laura and Chris joined him.

"No wonder Millard didn't want to call the police," said Jake slowly.

10

The phosphorescent slime seemed to fill the darkened compound. Making a bubbling, slithering sound, it was erupting from one of the tanks in a thick stream, slopping on to the wiry grass and oozing towards the perimeter wire, scorching the ground as it went.

"It looks different," Jake gasped as the security arc lights suddenly came on again. "Like it's about fifty times as big."

Laura and Chris jostled Jake for position at the window, gazing out incredulously. "It's kind of sinewy," Laura whispered. "With tentacles. Like a huge pulsating worm. Yuck!"

"But it's a chemical." Jake could hardly get the words out.

"It's more than a spill, for God's sake," said Laura slowly.

"The stuff must be about ten metres long – and still coming," muttered Chris.

Acidic steam rose from the pale, veined, worm-like thing that in the glare of the lights now seemed slightly transparent. Was something flowing through its veins? Jake wondered. And if so – what the hell could the liquid be?

Alarms began to sound as the toxic slime reached the wire. But this time the stuff made no attempt to burrow underneath. Instead the slime began to eat its way through in a bubbling haze and metal sparks flew as the wire parted.

Jake was badly shocked. This was some leak! A thin stream had turned into a tentacled monstrosity. What could have gone wrong? Was that why Millard had been so afraid?

"At least the slime doesn't need wire-cutters," muttered Laura.

Suddenly a group of staff in protective suits, helmets and visors hurried out of one of the pre-fabricated buildings and then came to a halt, staring helplessly, watching the slime ooze through the wire, bulbous and sinewy, with its pulsating veins.

Then one of them began to talk urgently into a mobile phone.

"Maybe we're going to be thrown to the slime,"

Jake suggested, and a wave of panic swept him. Was *that* why the police hadn't come? Was *that* why they had been locked in this squalid little room? Did the slime need to be fed? It was a ludicrous idea — wasn't it? Jake glanced at Laura and Chris, horrified by the growing terror in their eyes, knowing they were all having the same appalling thought.

Then they heard footsteps hurrying down the corridor and the door was unlocked and thrown open.

"This is an emergency," said a woman in protective clothing, pushing up her visor, looking devastated. "You have to get clear. There's been a major leak."

"Another one?" asked Chris. "The stuff seems to have a mind of its own."

"This leak's total."

"Can't you stop it?" asked Jake.

"There's been a complication."

"You mean, the stuff's out of control?" demanded Chris.

"We don't know what it's going to do."

"What is it?" asked Laura. "What *is* the slime?"

"It's a chemical substance. I can't tell you more than that."

Jake returned to the window. The slime seemed even more swollen than ever, a great bulbous stream which glistened and glowed, sliding over the road now, burning off the surface in a cloud of steam.

"You're going to let us out?"

"Yes. But I wouldn't stay around."

Laura was staring at the woman intently. "How dangerous is this chemical?"

"It's lethal, but I'm sure they'll have it under control in a very short time."

"Where's Millard?" asked Jake. "Is he going to be on the front line?"

"He's at home in bed but they've called him out."

"He'll have some explaining to do." Laura strode purposefully towards the door.

"He's good at that," said Jake bitterly. "Millard could explain anything away – even the end of the world."

"He might just have to do that," added Chris.

As soon as they stepped outside the stench of sulphur was overpowering, getting down their throats, making them gag. But gradually they found themselves getting used to the filthy smell and more able to concentrate on the horror of what was happening.

Jake, Chris and Laura were completely ignored, although a surprising number of Craven Marsh personnel were standing around, helplessly watching the slime's progress as it flowed endlessly out of one of the tanks, steam rising from its toxic surface.

A helicopter flew overhead, searchlights flashing, highlighting the bizarre scene as the molten, stinking slime continued to escape from the tank whose cover and valve must have burst open from the enormous pressure below.

Dozens of personnel were now running alongside the substance which, in the moonlight, seemed to have a grey-green sheen. In the helicopter's lights Jake could see the front of the slime was already consuming a row of ancient beach huts, a concrete pill-box and a winch. All were disintegrating in the deadly flow of acid.

"Let's get down to the beach," yelled Laura. "That'll be the fastest way home."

She began to run and Chris and Jake followed, keeping pace beside the evil-smelling substance which still showed no sign of diminishing as the tank continued to belch the stuff out.

Above them, stars shone and the moon bathed the slime in unearthly pallid light as it oozed over the pebbles, making a grating, shifting sound.

A pale grey dawn was slowly filtering the sky as another helicopter arrived, chattering overhead, its beam again picking out the boiling surface of the slime as it hit the waves in a burst of spray and steam.

"Don't get too near," yelled Laura, glancing back at Jake and Chris, not looking where she was going and then tripping and flailing, narrowly missing the slime. Jake gave a warning shout but Chris immediately ground to a halt, gasping for breath, his face pale and drawn.

Meanwhile the Craven Marsh staff ran on, shouting at each other, barely in control, panic spreading like an infection. Jake felt the same himself, heart thudding, his mouth so dry that he was continuously trying and failing to summon up saliva.

Then a man in protective clothing ran between him and the slime. "Don't get so near," he yelled at Jake. "You're too close."

The man pushed him away, staggered, tried to recover himself, failed, and then fell over an upturned dinghy, rolling into the path of the slime.

For a fraction of a second his eyes met Jake's. Then he was enveloped in a cloud of toxic steam, his protective suit eaten away, his features blackening, skin peeling, until the acid consumed him flesh and bone. Within minutes there was nothing left but a thin haze rising up into the dawn-streaked sky.

Laura and Chris stood with Jake, gazing down at where the man had once been, the filthy smell, more noxious than ever, filling their nostrils.

11

The slime was floating, half-submerged, on the waves. The grey dawn had dulled its phosphorescence and the substance was now dun-coloured, slowly drifting.

Just as Jake was wondering if the thing was dying, the slime began to move, heading out to sea, the toxic mist rising.

"It's complete," said Laura, who had been looking back up the beach. "There isn't any more to come."

The last of the slime swept past them and slid into the waves. Jake thought it now measured well over forty metres long.

Jake saw Millard walking down the pebbles, hunched in a dark overcoat, accompanied by a couple of film crews and a cluster of photographers. He looked like a wolf with a hungry pack.

Back on the road the fire engines, ambulances and police cars had drawn up, sirens still wailing, as well as a large number of vehicles belonging to more press and TV crews. Meanwhile, the helicopters were following the slime out to sea, their high-powered beams still playing.

"I don't reckon the slime's just a chemical that's leaked from its container," Jake said to Laura. "What if it was *deliberately* made to be actively aggressive?"

Laura simply gazed ahead without replying, leaving Chris to say, "The stuff's certainly got an appetite."

"For everything and anything in its path," added Jake.

"For God's sake, shut up!" yelled Laura. "Isn't the situation bad enough? Why do you two ghouls have to prattle on?"

"There's only one ghoul round here," said Jake shortly, "and it's swimming out to sea."

Millard turned to face the media. The smell of sulphur still hung heavily over the beach and Jake noticed that some of the reporters were looking ill.

Confident as ever, Millard turned to the cameras while Jake, Laura and Chris edged nearer, trying to overhear what he was saying.

"Once the substance is immersed in salt water for a certain length of time, the chemical shrinks and is rendered harmless."

"How long will that take?" asked a reporter suspiciously.

"I can't say," said Millard guardedly.

"Can't you be more specific than that?"

"I'm afraid not."

"What *is* the stuff?"

"An experiment."

"What kind of experiment?"

"This substance was being developed as a means of disposing of household waste and preventing landfill. But somehow the formula has developed a fault, causing the chemical to grow too quickly for the size of our containers."

"What are you going to do about it? Look what it's done to those beach huts."

"No great harm done. The owners will be compensated," Millard promised.

No one's mentioned what happened to the man in the protective suit, thought Jake. Maybe we were the only ones to see how he died. But he hadn't reckoned on Laura stepping towards the lights and cameras and whispering to one of the reporters.

Then she shouted, "Millard's lying!"

A couple of heavies began to push their way over to her. As they did so, both Jake and Chris moved forward protectively.

Meanwhile Laura continued: "A *lot* of harm's been done. A worker from Craven Marsh just fell into the slime and died a horrible death. I'm sure the stuff doesn't have anything to do with domestic waste."

"What's your name?" asked a reporter.

"Laura—" she began, but Millard was at her side.

"Just to make our lives even harder," he said smoothly, "these young people broke into our compound last night, apparently making some kind of ill-informed protest. None of our staff has been injured by the substance – of course no one has been killed – and the chemical most certainly *has* been developed for the disposal of household waste."

Now the cameras were focusing on Millard again and Jake was staggered at the enormous risk he was taking. Were his staff so loyal that they would automatically back up his propaganda? Or were the Craven Marsh workers so frightened of what they had become involved in that none of them dared open their mouth?

Millard was still talking to camera while Laura stood alone, unnoticed and seemingly dismissed. They just think she's some attention-seeking student, thought Jake. Shouldn't he and Chris try to convince them? But when Jake glanced at Chris he simply shrugged, realizing they had all lost the interest of the media.

"I must emphasize," Millard was saying, "that we have the situation perfectly under control. We're extremely sorry about what has happened, but there is absolutely no danger to the general public." He turned to watch the slime still heading out to sea. "I can see the chemical's decreasing in size already and there is *no* further danger."

It's impossible to see whether the stuff is decreasing or not, thought Jake. The light's too bad.

Laura returned to Chris and Jake. "It's hopeless," she whispered. "They won't listen to us."

Meanwhile, one of the reporters began to sum up the story to camera.

"It looks as if all's well that ends well with the chemical spill at Craven Marsh. The substance is now drifting out to sea and experts predict that the effect of the salt water will destroy the toxic material. At the moment, however, the chemical looks as if it's still about forty metres long. The Ministry of Defence spokesman, Andrew Millard, has apologized for the leak and categorically states that the emergency is over. This is Ray Coombs for News at Seven on the beach at Craven Marsh."

The camera crews began to pack up their equipment and the photographers headed back towards their vehicles.

Jake screwed up his eyes and gazed out at the horizon as the grey light of dawn began to spread. "I think it's turning," he said as the Craven Marsh workers milled past him, heading back to the research station.

"It can't be," gasped Laura.

"The slime's definitely heading back," Chris said urgently. "And it's not shrunk at all. In fact, I think the stuff's grown."

Jake glanced at Millard and his minders. A little pulse was again beating in Millard's temple as one of the TV reporters crunched over the pebbles towards him. "The thing's coming back," he shouted.

"Once the chemical reaches the beach the toxicity will have been reduced," Millard responded hurriedly, but he was no longer his usual cool, confident self.

"You said it would shrink." The reporter was incredulous.

"So it will."

"But when?"

Laura moved forward, but Jake grabbed her arm.

"Look."

Glancing back at the road, she saw that a convoy of army jeeps, armoured cars and trucks full of troops had drawn up, their engines ticking over.

Hurriedly, the TV crews ran back down the beach and started to set up their cameras again.

"Well?" persisted the reporter. "Why have the army shown up if there's no danger to anyone?"

"Just a precaution." There were beads of sweat standing out on Millard's forehead.

"What kind of precaution?"

For once Millard took some time to reply. "The army's here just in case the substance needs to be cleaned off the beach. We're very – environmentally conscious here at Craven Marsh."

"I take it the chemical can't be cleaned off human beings, Mr Millard. Is that the real problem? Just how many workers have you lost?"

"As I told you – none at all. And there's no question of—"

"Suppose we talk to some of them—" The reporter broke off as a shout went up.

"The stuff's changing course again!" yelled someone.

"And I'm sure it's getting bigger, not smaller," muttered Laura.

Jake gazed out to sea. The slime certainly looked bigger and was now heading up the coast towards Shingleton.

"Let's go," said Laura.

"Where?" asked Chris.

"Back to Shingleton. Where else? The slime's travelling fast. Suppose it attacks the town?"

"The TV crews are coming over. This could be the chance we've been waiting for – the chance Millard's been so afraid we might take." Jake was all for grabbing the opportunity, but Laura wasn't so sure.

"An interview could take too much time, and time's something we haven't got."

Just then they heard the roaring of engines as the army convoy began to move up the coast road.

Laura was already stumbling over the pebbles towards the road when one of the TV reporters shouted. "Can we have an interview, Laura? Can I speak to you now? We need to talk to you and you want to talk to us, don't you, Laura?"

The cry was picked up by the other reporters. "We need to talk to you, Laura!" The reporters began to hurry towards her, followed by the camera crews, while the slime still swam lazily up the coast.

"I haven't got time," shouted Laura. "If you want to talk, come to Shingleton."

Jake and Chris raced after her and soon they were jogging along the roadside as the military vehicles continued to thunder past.

12

Ten minutes later a small van slowed down and kept pace with them as they ran.

Jake glanced inside to see a young woman and a jumble of recording equipment on the front seat.

"I'm Gill Crosby," she shouted, winding down her window. "Radio Chatham FM. Can I give you a lift?"

She skidded to a halt as the military convoy continued to rumble past and another couple of helicopters flew overhead, one of which was marked AIR-SEA RESCUE.

"We've got to get to Shingleton," panted Laura.

"You can talk into my tape recorder as we go."

They jumped into the van with Laura in the front

seat and Chris and Jake sitting uncomfortably on the floor at the back.

"Go for it," said Gill Crosby, handing her a mike.

With considerable eloquence, Laura began with the incidents that Jake had witnessed and went on to their "protest" invasion of Craven Marsh, the escape of the slime and the death of the worker.

"So they're doing a massive cover-up," said Gill, when Laura had finished. "I've often wondered about that place. This is a real coup for me. After all, we're only a small local radio station. Once we've broadcast the tape we can flog the story right across the media."

Suddenly the army truck in front of them came to a grinding halt and Gill stamped on the brakes.

Two young soldiers walked slowly up to the window of the van. Both were armed.

As Gill rolled down the window, one of them asked for her name.

"Gill Crosby. Radio Chatham."

"And your passengers?"

Chris made the introductions.

The soldier glanced at the tape recorder. "There's been a D-notice slapped on Craven Marsh. You can't report anything that hasn't been vetted. I'm going to have to ask you to hand over that tape, together with any notes you may have taken."

"No chance," said Gill tersely.

"What *is* a D-notice?" asked Jake.

"It's censorship," she explained bitterly. "Something that the government can impose during a national crisis."

"So despite everything Millard said, this *is* a national crisis," said Chris.

"The tapes, please," said the soldier with gathering impatience.

Gill wound up the window.

To Jake's amazement, the soldier raised his gun, and for a moment he waited for him to shoot. This can't be happening, he thought. This is England, not eastern Europe.

Instead, the soldier stepped back – and smashed the window of the van with the stock of his gun.

The glass fell in, covering Gill with fragments.

"Now let's have the tapes."

"No chance," she repeated, seemingly unmoved. "What the hell do you think you're doing?"

He then flung the driver's door open and grabbed at the tape recorder. So did Laura and Gill, their hands closing over the cassette. There was an undignified tugging match until Jake leant over and tried to snatch the tape himself.

The soldier brought down the butt of his rifle on his wrist and Jake howled with pain while the soldier seized the tape recorder and threw it on the ground outside.

"You've damaged my property," yelled Gill Crosby.

"It isn't your property any more." He gazed steadily ahead, not making eye contact with any of them.

Jake was still nursing his hand.

"You OK, Jake?" asked Laura.

"Sort of."

"If he's done any damage—"

"I haven't," said the soldier blandly. "In any case, you were refusing to obey an order. This is an emergency – and we have to take special measures."

"The TV crews filmed the slime." Jake winced. "So you're too late."

"The materials won't be transmitted. Now we're going to search your van for any other recording equipment."

"I want to see your Commanding Officer," said Gill. She was furious. "You've destroyed my property as well as assaulted one of my passengers."

"It was unavoidable."

Ignoring further protests, the soldiers checked through the contents of the vehicle, slammed the doors and walked back to their truck.

The convoy began to move off again but then came to another abrupt halt.

Jake glanced out of the window. "At this rate, Shingleton could be wiped out before we get there." Panic rose in him when he thought of Dad and Ben. Everything was out of control and there was nothing they could do. He felt like the workers at Craven Marsh as they had helplessly watched the escape of the toxic slime. But why was he just assuming that, he thought suddenly. He'd seen the slime in its infancy and the stuff had nearly killed him. Then, when they'd broken into Craven Marsh, they'd seen the slime in all its awesome maturity. There was no point in feeling helpless. They *had* to do something.

"Have you got relatives in Shingleton?" asked Laura, and Gill shook her head.

"No, thank God." She paused and then pulled something out of her back pocket. "The soldiers weren't very thorough, were they?"

"What's that?"

"It's a little machine I use for dictating notes," said Gill. She turned back to Laura. "Do you mind repeating all that again? It won't be broadcast quality, but at least we'll have a record – if—" She suddenly seemed at a loss for words.

"If anything happens to me," finished Laura.

By the time she had retold the story, Jake and Chris were getting increasingly agitated, particularly when the convoy ground to a halt yet again.

"We'd be faster on foot," said Jake, unable to bear the mounting tension any longer. He had to get out. He had to *do* something.

"Let's go for it," agreed Chris. "It's only about half a mile now."

"Best of luck," said Gill. "And for God's sake, be careful."

They jumped out, running down the side of the road, past the trucks full of troops who gazed at them suspiciously but made no attempt to stop them.

After a few minutes, they understood why the convoy was moving so erratically. A stream of vehicles was crawling away from Shingleton and a small builder's van had overturned on a corner. A breakdown truck was gradually winching it upright while the driver, who had a cut head, was sitting by the roadside.

As Laura, Jake and Chris ran past him, he yelled out, "What the hell do you think you're doing?"

"Heading for Shingleton," gasped Jake.

"Go back the other way."

"Why?" demanded Chris.

"There's some filthy chemical stuff in the sea, polluting everything and stinking like hell itself."

"What's it doing?"

"Nothing. What should it be doing?" The man looked puzzled. " It's floating around outside the harbour."

Jake breathed a sigh of relief.

"So why is everyone leaving?"

"The smell's incredible. It's all over town. I had trouble breathing. A lot of people are trying to get out and I took that corner too fast."

"So it's just the smell—" began Laura.

The man shuddered. "I can smell it on my clothes now. The stuff's revolting."

"Wasn't there any warning?" asked Chris.

"Just a newsflash about a chemical leak at Craven Marsh and that everything was under control. Do they reckon they've got all that stinking mess in the water under control?"

"Is that all they said?"

"The police went round with loudspeaker vans saying the stuff had leaked into the sea and no one was to go near it." He paused. "There's a rumour the Royal Navy's on the way."

"Are you going back?" asked Laura.

"No chance. I was heading for my mother's place in Folkestone. When I've got this lot sorted, I'm going to grab a taxi."

"Don't you need hospital treatment?"

"All I need to do is to get a long way from Shingleton. I've never felt so trapped."

There was a crash as the breakdown truck righted the van and a group of soldiers arrived to push the battered vehicle on to the track that ran beside the beach.

At last the traffic began to move again in both directions and the three of them ran on. Jake was boiling with rage. What right did the government have to withhold information? The people of Shingleton could be in terrible danger. Secrecy always led to disaster. Just look at what had happened at Craven Marsh.

Eventually they reached the headland, climbing the steep slope and then down the other side towards Shingleton. Only two names beat in Jake's mind. Dad. Ben. Dad. Ben. Dad – he couldn't get the drum-like rhythm out of his head.

There was still no wind and the sea, glinting in the strong light, looked innocent and unruffled. Running on short-cropped turf, the sun rising in a blue sky, Jake could hear the plaintive cries of the gulls and feel the sun warm on his back. Dad. Ben. Dad. Ben—

Suddenly Laura, who was now slightly in front, came to an abrupt halt, gazing down. Jake almost bumped into her, hearing Chris gasping for breath behind him.

Then he saw what Laura was staring at. The slime had grown to at least double its size and was now about eighty metres long, wallowing in the swell just short of the harbour, a bulbous grey-green, with blue veins. There was something increasingly menacing about the way its huge bulk rose and fell with the waves – almost as if it was waiting. Gulls rose in a cloud and then flew away, crying despondently. A slight breeze blew the smell of sulphur towards them, much more pungent than before.

"Whatever's made it grow like that?" whispered Chris.

"Fish?" suggested Laura. "Weed? Something in the sea, anyway."

"What'll happen if it lands?" asked Jake, expressing all their thoughts.

"Maybe it won't," said Chris hopefully. "The slime seems to be getting all the nourishment it needs from the sea."

"Let's hope you're right." Laura shuddered as she gazed down at the wallowing mass. "Please God you're right," she muttered.

13

There were barriers and traffic cones across the road leading into Shingleton where a number of trestle tables were piled high with square white boxes.

Very few civilians were going into the town, but those that were each received a box, given out by the soldiers.

The military were drawing up their vehicles on the far side of the harbour and were standing in groups, as if waiting for a briefing. The convoy was still slowly arriving from the coast road, while other vehicles, including dozens of cars and vans, were equally slowly leaving the town in a continuous stream.

"What's in those boxes?" Chris was apprehensive.

Someone was dragging out a weird-looking mask.

"I know what they are," said Laura.

"Well, don't hold out on us!" snapped Jake, and Laura looked hurt and almost tearful.

"I'm not," she said, her voice shaking, and Chris put his arm round her protectively.

"Don't start bullying Laura."

Stung by his criticism, Jake almost lost control. He would have liked to hit Chris and had a satisfying mental image of slapping him hard across the face with the back of his hand.

But in reality Jake only clenched his fists. "Sorry, Laura," he apologized.

"They're gas masks," she rapped out. "What else could they be?"

Again the breeze wafted in their direction and the filthy smell filled their nostrils.

As they hurried on towards the harbour the noxious stink of sulphur got much worse. When they arrived, Jake approached a sergeant who was behind one of the trestle tables.

"What about everybody in the town? Are they being given masks, too?"

"We've got a truck up there now," the sergeant said impatiently.

"Are you going to have enough to go round?"

"There are more supplies coming in. But there may be an evacuation later."

"Why?" demanded Chris.

"You may have noticed there's a large chemical spill in the sea," said the sergeant sarcastically. "Or do you think we've been visited by a friendly sea monster? I can tell you the spill's highly toxic."

"How do you put the masks on?"

"There are instructions in the box." Then he seemed to relent. "Got family up there then?"

"We all have," said Jake.

"I should tell them to pack up and get out now like most folks are. Some of the schools are being opened in Seaton as temporary shelters." The sergeant paused and glanced out to sea. "I've got this feeling we haven't got much time left."

"Let's make contact with our folks and arrange to meet up again," suggested Chris.

"OK." Laura turned to Jake. "How about you?"

He nodded, still wondering what would happen if the slime came ashore. "We need to see this through," he muttered. "We've got inside information."

"Let's meet at two outside St Catherine's," said Laura.

Jake glanced down at his watch and saw that it was just gone twelve. For a moment he wondered about the wisdom of splitting up for so long. Then his concern for Dad and Ben overwhelmed his fears.

* * *

The streets were full of gas-masked figures and Jake felt as if he had arrived in an alien city – except that he was now wearing a mask too. He could hear his own breathing, the sweat was pouring into his eyes and he had an increasing sense of being trapped. Although the smell of sulphur was less intense, the feeling of claustrophobia was unbearable. The eye-pieces kept steaming up and he began to see Shingleton through a fog of condensation, with dream-like people shifting and drifting before him. Even the buildings looked insubstantial.

When he arrived home, Dad was calm but Ben seemed slightly drunk. There were two gas masks on the table, but the smell was not so bad inside the cottage and Jake took his own off with considerable relief.

He was alarmed. Jake had only seen Ben drunk once before and that was at Christmas. Normally his uncle was level-headed and resilient.

"I thought you'd be at college," Dan muttered.

"With that thing oozing about out there?"

"Where the hell's the navy? Why don't they come and blow that filth out of the sea?"

Ben turned to Jake. "Can't you persuade your dad to do the sensible thing and pack a suitcase?"

"I'm not going anywhere," said Dan. "Not while the *Lucky Strike*'s in danger. She's our livelihood, in case you've forgotten."

"The boat's insured. Why don't we drive down to

Seaton and see if Maggie will put us up for a few nights?" His voice was slightly slurred.

"No way." Dan was as stubborn as ever. "I don't know what's got into you. Never seen you running scared like this before."

"That thing's getting bigger all the time."

"As for these gas masks…" Dan continued.

Then the telephone rang and Ben grabbed the receiver, seeming to sober up. He listened and muttered something inaudible before putting it down.

"Who was that?" asked Jake.

"Charlie Mason. He wants to know if we're going to move the *Strike*."

"You bet we are," said Dan.

The trawler was on a jetty that was just beyond the harbour where the mooring fees were expensive.

"I'm surprised you haven't been down there," said Jake.

"I was waiting for you, son. But before you condescended to show up, we were told not to go near any of the jetties."

"On whose authority?"

"The police gave out the instruction from a loud-speaker van." Dan scowled. "Normally I'm a law-abiding citizen. But you can kiss that idea goodbye. I'm going to save our property."

"Wait a minute, Dad," interrupted Jake. "There's a newsflash."

A blurred shot of the harbour at Shingleton came up, looking workaday and peaceful under the summer sun. Then Jake saw a grey-green tentacle sliding over the top of the wall, searching for a grip.

"It's landing," yelled Jake, the panic hammering in his head, wishing that he and Laura had never decided to split up. He knew the idea had been a bad mistake. Looking at his watch, Jake saw the time was just after twelve-thirty. Anything could happen in an hour and a half.

"Now we've got to get out," said Ben. "What more proof do you need?"

"I'm not being forced out," Dan insisted.

"What's the matter with you? Why don't you try and get real?"

"Shut up, both of you," muttered Jake.

"– a chemical experiment gone wrong," said the reporter's urgent voice-over. "Immersion in the sea appears to have made the substance grow rather than shrink, as claimed. The material is highly toxic and has drifted down to Shingleton, having leaked out of the MOD research station at Craven Marsh. Now the substance is slowly sliding over the harbour wall."

The slime was still about eighty metres long with huge, sinewy tentacles. Even on the small TV Jake could see its pulsating veins, particularly noticeable in the tentacles which made a slithering, sucking sound as they gripped the ancient stone blocks of the harbour.

Then one of the tentacles lazily stretched out to a small kiosk which sold bait for amateur fishermen. Almost immediately the rusty metal began to melt and a motorbike that was leaning against the kiosk burst into spluttering flame.

"So it can burn as well as melt," muttered Jake incredulously. Then he turned to Ben. "Didn't you do some kind of scientific research when you were abroad?" he demanded. "Have you seen anything like this before?"

"Slime wasn't my line," snapped Ben. "I don't know anything about chemical spills."

"Chemical spill, my arse!" exclaimed Dan. "What the hell are we going to do?" For once he was at a loss.

"Like I told you," said Ben. "Get out fast."

But none of them moved, their eyes on the screen.

There were a number of cars and vans parked along the harbour wall, and as the toxic slime stroked a battered Ford, a sheet of vivid orange flame rose, igniting other vehicles. Then the fire spread to a shed.

Jake watched in amazement. This was like an old-fashioned monster movie. But it was for real.

The reporter's voice was lost in the roaring of the blaze while the camera tracked back until all that could be seen was a dense spiral of black smoke. Alarms began to sound and people scattered for cover.

"I'm going to take the *Lucky Strike* round to Longshore," said Dan. "And that's *all* I'm doing – at least for the moment." He seemed to take comfort from focusing exclusively on the trawler, but when Jake glanced at Ben he could see that he understood the full implications of the situation, just as Jake did. Unless the authorities did something, Shingleton could be wiped out.

The TV screen showed people milling about in the streets, hardly able to believe what was happening as more vehicles caught fire.

The army seemed as confused as the general public, only managing to clear the way through the crowd with some difficulty for a couple of fire engines.

Meanwhile the grey-green bulbous mass was still oozing over the harbour wall, not in the least affected by the blaze. In fact, the flames seemed to bounce off the slimy, sinewy surface.

Jake glanced at his watch and saw that there was still an hour to go before they'd all arranged to meet outside St Catherine's. Suppose the slime began to invade the streets and he couldn't reach Laura? Suppose – Jake tried to stop himself thinking.

"I'm going down to the moorings," said Dan, and Ben nodded. He seemed calmer now and had completely sobered up. "What about you, Jake?"

"I'll join you down there."

Surprisingly, his father was, once again, understanding. Had he really not known him all these years? Not really tried to see into his mind. "Laura?"

"I've got to make sure she's safe."

"I'd have done the same for your mother." He sounded bitter. "A long time ago."

"Be very careful," said Ben. "We'll wait at Longshore for you."

"OK," said Jake, gazing back at the TV screen which showed a helicopter hovering, drenching the blaze with water, while the long white hoses of the fire engines quivered on the quayside, also shooting jets of water at the flames.

The reporter was gabbling now and barely audible. "What's happening at Shingleton has all the makings of a national disaster. The whole of the quayside is now ablaze and the slime is still advancing, untouched by the fire, gradually dragging itself out of the sea and beginning to slither up Ship Street."

Dan came over to Jake, gripping his shoulder. "You get Laura and bring her down to Longshore – and her family if they'll come. I've got this feeling we may need to put to sea."

"You've always felt safer there," said Jake, "haven't you, Dad?"

He nodded and they embraced. Then Jake did the same to his uncle and he could see tears in Ben's eyes. Was that the drink? He rather thought not. Jake had never realized just how close the three of them had become.

14

Laura's parents owned a gift shop not far from the harbour, and as Jake raced down the narrow streets, desperately concerned for her safety, he met hundreds of people going the other way. As he tried to push past them, Jake felt their raw panic. The smell of sulphur, however, seemed a little less overpowering – or was he just getting used to it? Some of the crowd were wearing masks, but others, like himself, clearly thought that the stench was more bearable than the claustrophobia.

Then a hollow booming sound began, repeated over and over again.

Jake caught sight of Bill Farley, who repaired boats near the harbour slipway, and yelled at him: "What's happening?"

"The army are firing at the chemical."

"With any result?"

"Not a lot. That stuff's set the harbour alight. I wouldn't go down there, Jake."

"Where is it now?"

"Still oozing up Ship Street."

"Any casualties?"

"Dozens. They didn't stand a chance."

"Do you know Laura Knights?"

"Yes – I saw her dad loading up their car. Said he was going to try and get out through Moorcroft Place, but I bet that'll be jammed solid now."

Without replying, Jake ran on, still pushing his way through the ever-thickening crowd.

"Where're you going?" yelled Bill.

"Where do you think?" shouted Jack over his shoulder. "To get Laura, of course."

"This isn't the time to play the hero."

"What better time could there be?"

The quayside was in chaos. The fire appliances were still aiming jets of water at the burning vehicles and sheds; a black plume of smoke continued to rise and the army were firing at the slime from behind their armoured vehicles with high velocity rifles. They seemed to be having no effect whatsoever.

Jake felt deeply afraid. There was something incredibly primitive about the slime, impervious as it was to fire and bullets. It was as if the stuff was invincible.

As the black smoke on the quayside cleared for a moment, Jake saw the stonework had been deeply affected by the acid and was gouged into grotesque shapes.

Meanwhile, just discernible above the noise of the firing and shouted instructions, was the sound of the slime: a heavy slithering that sent a chill right through him.

He arrived at the gift shop only to find Chris outside, looking apprehensive.

"What are you doing here?" Jake asked with sudden, all too obvious irritation.

"Waiting for Laura."

"Where is she?"

"Helping her dad load up the car."

"Why aren't you with them?"

"Laura wanted me to look out for you." Chris sounded hurt now as well as afraid, and Jake felt ashamed. "You seen how the thing's grown?" Chris looked overwhelmed, as if he was barely coping. "Where's your gas mask?" he asked.

"Where's yours? I'm beginning to get used to the smell anyway." Jake didn't want to admit how trapped he had felt wearing the thing.

"We shouldn't hang around here too long," said Chris. "Fires will be starting all over the town. My parents are going to try and get out over the headland – like Laura's."

"That may be difficult," said Jake. "I've been told

all the streets are jammed with traffic. Hasn't there been any news about an official evacuation?"

"Not that I've heard. So what are we going to do?" Chris sounded uncharacteristically dependent on him.

We've got to be united, Jake thought to himself. Somehow.

"Dan and Ben are taking the trawler round to Longshore."

"That's an idea." Chris suddenly looked hopeful. "Would there be room for all of us?"

"Yes," said Jake. "But we've got to get down to the jetty and that could be difficult."

Just then, Laura came out of the shop, looking haggard. "Thank God," she said. "I've been so worried about you. We should never have split up."

Laura hugged him and for the first time in a long while Jake felt needed.

A cloud of steam rose over the rooftops and there was a terrible screaming sound which suddenly stopped. Jake could hardly believe what was happening. Shingleton had been his home ever since he had been born and the town was so familiar he knew every brick, every stone, every road, every building. Nothing had ever really happened in Shingleton. Now it was like the end of the world had arrived.

The familiar slithering sound was getting louder and to his horror Jake realized that rather than disappearing over the hill the slime was coming back down again.

There was an explosion and the buildings round them shook as a sheet of flame crackled and roared, blotting out the sun. Rolling black smoke was blown towards them while a crowd of people began to run down the hill, back to the harbour, some falling and being trampled by those behind them.

Laura's parents appeared in the doorway. "We're ready," Mrs Knights shouted at them, her eyes glazed with fear. "The car's loaded."

Assuming Laura was following, the Knights went back into the shop again.

Then Jake saw his father stumbling down the hill.

"Dad!" he yelled. "What the hell are you doing? I thought you were heading for the *Lucky Strike*."

"So I should be. But I'm looking for Ben. He disappeared into the crowd."

They were now shouting to make themselves heard above the sound of the slithering, squelching of the advancing slime and the screams of the crowd as they pushed their way past them.

Dan came to a halt, leaning gasping against the shop front. "Why don't you come with me? Like now?"

"Why not?" said Chris.

Jake glanced at Laura. "What about it?"

"I can't. I've got to go with my parents—" She was utterly confused, not knowing what to do.

"Let's get in the shop." Jake dragged Laura in with Dan and Chris close behind as the blunt head of the slime rounded the corner, monstrous, steaming and vile-smelling.

As Chris slammed the door they ran to the window to watch the stuff pass, while its sulphurous stink made them all choke.

"We should go upstairs," yelled Dan. "If that thing touches the shop-front, we'll all be in meltdown."

Laura led the way up and into her bedroom where they once again gazed out on to the street. The slime, which now rose in height as far as the ground-floor windows, took just over five minutes to pass and Jake felt those minutes were the most terrifying in his whole life. There was something so repulsive about the dreadful slithering, and so nauseating about the pulsating veins in the grey-green body that it took all his self-control not to cry out in disgust.

Soon the slime filled the length of the street, and whatever its body brushed against was scorched or melted while the cobbles smoked beneath its acidic weight.

But worse was to come. Suddenly Jake saw flattened, squeezed-dry corpses caught up in the monstrous coils.

"It's sucked the blood out of them," whispered Laura.

"So that's why it came ashore," said Chris. "Maybe it just made do with the nutrients in the sea but now it needs human nourishment."

"So what *is* this thing that started off as a chemical and then became – a – what?"

"Maybe it was specially bred." Dan was thinking aloud.

"What do you mean, Dad?" demanded Jake.

"Suppose the slime was bred to melt and burn and kill," Dan continued.

"You mean like some kind of – of weapon?" said Chris.

"It could be that." Dan was hesitant. "We should have got rid of Craven Marsh a long time ago. This is worse than any of the rumours that used to fly around."

"Do you think the thing's got a mind?" asked Jake, but his father didn't reply.

"Or could someone have programmed the slime?" Laura said suddenly. "Suppose all this is a test run?"

"That's ridiculous!" But Chris looked as if he wasn't sure of anything.

Dan merely shrugged, staring intently down at the slithering coils which seemed endless.

Mr Knights appeared on the landing, gasping for breath. "We're off," he said. "Get moving."

"There are too many of us," said Laura. "You and Mum get away – as soon as the streets are clear. We'll make it on foot."

"We can't leave you!" He was horrified, unable to believe what she was saying.

"We'll be all right."

"Laura—" Her father was desperate. "You've *got* to come with us."

The slime had passed, leaving a trail of stinking debris and a cindery trail. But they could still hear the dreadful slithering sound.

"We'll be all right, Dad," Laura repeated. "Just go."

"Wait a minute," said Jake. "I've got an idea. Could you take my father as far as the beach on the other side of the headland – then he can make it to our trawler."

"I've got a better idea," said Dan. "Park the car at the jetty and we'll all make it out in the *Lucky Strike*."

"We'll join you later," said Laura.

"Don't be a fool!" Her father was almost in tears. "We'll all manage to squeeze in somehow."

"Chris wants to contact his parents," Laura insisted. "We don't want him to try that on his own."

"I can't let you—"

"You'll have to," she said firmly. "I promise you – we won't be long."

"Come on," said Dan, taking Mr Knights' arm. "They'll be careful. They're not kids any more."

Once again Jake was surprised by his father. Surprised – and grateful.

Unwillingly, Mr Knights allowed himself to be steered downstairs. He was still protesting as they reached the ground floor.

"Best of luck," shouted Dan, and Jake felt a rush of love and affection. At least *his* father thought he could cope as an adult.

"We need to stick together," said Laura.

"But what can we do?" Chris was uneasy.

"I don't know – but I just have this strong feeling that even if they do get the slime under control there's going to be a cover-up."

"You're right," said Jake. "We need to suss out what the slime really is. What it's really meant for."

There was still an acidic steam coming off the damaged cobblestones outside and wherever the shops and houses had been grazed by the slime there were enormous singe marks. Luckily nothing nearby had caught fire, but the roaring of flames could be heard further up the hill.

"Let's go to the attic," said Laura. "You can see right across the harbour. We can get more of an idea about what's going on."

Chris looked upset and for a moment Jake thought he was ready to pull out. Then he realized how selfish he was being. "Where are your parents?" he asked.

"I told them to leave in the car with my younger brother," he said bleakly. "And that I'd make it out on foot. Of course they raised hell, but I needed to be with you two."

With Laura more likely, Jake thought. "OK," he spoke aloud. "It's the three of us against the slime." Jake was full of resentment, but he knew he would have to accept that Chris was here to stay.

As they gazed across the rooftops from the attic window, Jake saw the devastation was far greater than he had thought. The harbour was now a blackened ruin. On the far side a car showroom was burning and the blaze had spread to the Mariners' Arms next door.

The fire brigade, now with more engines, were trying to put out the fires, and Jake could hear sirens on the coast road. He suspected they were having enormous difficulties in getting through the traffic which was now likely to be grid-locked. Helicopters flew overhead and he saw a Royal Navy destroyer standing off-shore. Military vehicles were everywhere and armed soldiers and police were waiting in the square beside the harbour, anticipating the reappearance of the slime.

Further away, to the right, near a strip of shingle beach, a queue was forming outside a

Baptist chapel. Dimly Jake could hear the sound of singing:

Fierce raged the tempest o'er the deep
Watch did thine anxious servants keep
But thou was wrapped in guileless sleep
Calm and still.

The voices rose powerfully over the organ.

Jake couldn't see the slime which must be exploring the streets to the south-west of the town where the view was blocked by deserted warehouses. He realized, however, that if the slime did re-emerge on the quayside, the deadly stuff would destroy the chapel in seconds. He wondered whether Laura's parents and his father had reached safety and, for the first time in his life, Jake began to pray.

Overhead, the sky remained a brilliant blue, but acrid flames from the burning buildings were shooting up, accompanied by great gouts of black smoke.

The stench, now mingling with the smell of burning, was still strong.

"What are we going to do?" he asked aloud. "Does anyone speak slime?"

Neither Chris nor Laura replied and Jake realized that despite all their grand plans, none of them had the slightest idea what to do next.

Then they saw the slime emerge again, at the far end of the harbour, moving more slowly, oozing past the blaze. Was it slowing up, Jake wondered in sudden hope? He could see that the thing was heavily pulsating and its veins were rich with gore.

"Could it be dying?" asked Chris tentatively.

As if hypnotized, the soldiers stared at the slime which had now slithered to a halt.

"I think it's gorged itself so much that now it's having a siesta," said Laura.

"Attention!" came a command over a PA system. "All civilians are to leave the harbour area immediately. I repeat, all civilians are to leave the harbour area immediately!"

Police began herding the helpless milling crowd back towards the town, while the hymn singing broke off and the congregation left the chapel without a hint of panic, as if they had acquired an inner strength.

Still the slime lay quivering.

Meanwhile the instructions continued: "We are about to detonate explosives. It is essential to keep clear. I repeat – we are about to detonate explosives. It is essential to keep clear."

A line of troops moved across the car park and took up position a few metres from where the toxic slime had come to rest.

"Do you think they're going to attach explosives to the thing?" wondered Laura.

"If they do, someone's going to end up with slime all over their face," said Jake.

Ten minutes passed in frantic activity until the troops withdrew too.

Having been pushed back by the police, the crowd stood and watched while TV crews began to set themselves up behind piles of hastily erected sandbags. The cameras focused on the slime which was now completely still.

The troops had at last brought a real sense of authority to the harbour and the crowd was quiet, still, visibly reassured. There was a feeling of purpose, and even the smoking ruins seemed less threatening.

Then the hymn singing began again:

Oh sacred spirit, who didst brood
Upon the chaos dark and rude
Who bad'st its angry tumult cease
And gavest light and life and—

"Silence, please," came the order. "Absolute silence."

The troops waited while an officer scanned the slime with his binoculars.

A baby cried and a couple of dogs began to bark, one set off by the other.

The tide was going out, mud and sand

stretching out to the waves. Seagulls wheeled over the harbour, and their dismal cries seemed like a lament.

The slime was still motionless as the officer adjusted his headset. He seemed to be doing some kind of countdown.

The explosion came as an anticlimactic thud, but the dust cloud was dense. They waited impatiently as it hazed away.

"My God," breathed Jake. "What a filthy mess."

There was slime everywhere, slopped over vehicles, the twisted harbour wall, the road, shop fronts and burnt-out vehicles.

There was a slow hissing sound, accompanied by the plaintive cries of the gulls.

A feeble cheer went up and then the silence resumed.

Eventually, the PA system spluttered to life. "Do not approach the chemical. I repeat – do *not* approach the chemical. Remain where you are. Please remain exactly where you are."

The bits of slime were quivering, but Jake was sure that was only due to the force of the explosion. Was the emergency over? He felt deeply relieved, but there was something else. A sense of anticlimax and a feeling that the power was back in the hands of the authorities. They'd been cut out – just like the slime had been cut up by the force of the explosion.

Now they'd never know the secrets behind the creation of the chemical.

The hissing increased in volume and there was also a strange sighing sound. Then a gull settled on a piece of slime just as the hymn singing began again:

> *Loving shepherd of thy sheep*
> *Keep thy lamb in safety keep*
> *Nothing can thy power withstand*
> *None can pluck me from thy hand.*

Jake was watching the gull and then he looked away, seeing the supervising officer picking his way through the pulsating shreds. When he had reached the centre of the car park he gave the crowd a thumbs up, and cheers and applause, swelling in volume, began to echo around the harbour.

The officer turned, gave another thumbs-up sign to the explosives team and then began to walk slowly back towards his companions.

When Jake glanced back the gull had gone. But the slime was covered in burnt feathers.

"There's a piece on our window." Chris's voice was tense, but it was only small, draped over the sill and fluttering slightly in the light sea-breeze.

He opened the window slowly, but Jake grabbed his shoulder and dragged him away.

"Don't touch it, you prat!"

"Get your hands off me—"

Chris pushed Jake away while Laura, picking up an ancient tennis racquet, managed to hook the slime, bring it in and drop it on to the attic floor.

It lay there. Pulsating.

As they stared there was a strangled scream from outside which swelled until it became a mass cry of terror. Rushing back to the window they saw that the officer had fallen to the ground, his foot trapped by a slither of slime. As he rolled over, Jake saw the stuff burning through his boot.

Gradually the slime rose up the officer's leg, wrapping itself around his thigh. Screaming with agony, the officer flailed from side to side as the deadly acid seared his flesh to the bone. Within seconds he had been completely eaten away.

"There are hundreds of them," whispered Laura.

The particles of slime were all beginning to pulsate.

"They're growing—" muttered Jake, and then as Laura cried out he turned back to see that their own piece of slime was bubbling and pulsating on the scorched floorboards.

"Get it back on the racquet," yelled Laura, but Chris only gazed down, rooted to the spot.

Jake knelt on the floor and poked at the slime very gingerly with the racquet until some of the strands began to clutch at the strings. The faint smell was becoming increasingly pungent and the racquet began to melt.

Jake threw both racquet and slime out of the window, watching it hurtle to the street below.

As they gazed down at the harbour, they saw that dozens of different pieces of slime were beginning to expand until soon each was the size of a small dog.

"Seems like the army made a bit of a balls-up," said Chris.

"They've created hundreds of them." Laura was incredulous.

"This isn't Shingleton any more," gasped Jake. "This is Slime City."

15

"Once the slime was split into segments, each bit became a separate slime," said Laura.

"So what happens if you explode them all over again?" asked Jake. "Does their molecular structure mean that those bits would individually grow to the same size as the original? Because if that's the case, we're looking at extinction."

"It's a possibility," said Laura miserably.

"I think Laura could be right," Chris volunteered.

"I'm glad you two are in such agreement," muttered Jake.

Outside, chaos had broken out again as the crowds began to run, desperate to get away from the writhing slime segments that were even now slopping their way across the square and beyond.

As the pieces slithered into the path of the stampeding crowd, some people went down, eaten away voraciously by the acid. But as more people began to run back up the hill Laura called down to a middle-aged couple.

"Where are you going?"

"To the bus station. The police say the army's organizing transport out."

"How can they do that?" yelled Chris.

"I don't know, but it's our only chance."

"Let's join them," said Jake. "It could be our only chance, too."

As they ran up the steep, cobbled streets, Jake was wondering how soon the ever-growing particles of slime would be all over the town.

As people began to push past them, Laura, Chris and Jake increased their speed, conscious that if they didn't get ahead of the crowd they would never reach the bus station, let alone board a bus. Raw panic was sweeping the streets. The crowd pushed and shoved and jostled until it was clear only the fittest would survive.

Jake, Laura and Chris soon became separated. Several times Jake was almost pushed to the ground. Somehow he recovered himself, trying to keep on his feet, shoving at other people as much as they shoved at him. Tempers flared and as they rounded a corner Jake was hurled against a stone wall, jarring his shoulder and sending waves of pain all over his body.

Why had they been stupid enough to stay in Shingleton? They should all have gone to the *Lucky Strike*. At least he could have been with Dad. And what about Ben? Where was he? The thoughts jostled painfully in his head, as savage as the crowd.

His shoulder still aching, Jake plunged on, searching for the others and then seeing Chris caught up in a mass of people, all of whom were struggling to avoid being crushed against the wall of the post office.

Diving in, struggling to reach him, Jake spotted Laura who had fallen and was lying on the cobbles. The crowd had obviously made some attempt to avoid her, but pressure from behind would soon make that impossible.

Jake put his head down and charged, pushing people aside and then fending them off with his fists. Eventually he reached Laura, grabbing at her just as she was trying to stagger to her feet. Then a woman with a couple of young children ran into them and they all fell over in a heap with Jake underneath, kicking and struggling to get free, his face being ground into the cobblestones.

He heard Laura cry out and guessed he must have kicked her.

Jake was still struggling to get up when a man stumbled over him and fell, grinding him down yet again. Kicking and thrashing, he desperately tried to free himself and rolled over. Conscious of kicking someone else, he prayed it wasn't Laura.

Then he gave a howl of pain as someone grabbed his arms and pulled him backwards, scraping his skin on the cobbles, dragging him clear and into a doorway where Laura was already sitting, her face bloodied and torn, sobbing with fear.

When Jake looked up he could see Chris standing over him, gasping, his shoulders heaving and his eyes dilated.

"Did you pull me clear?" Jake panted.

Chris nodded.

"And me," choked Laura.

Jake got to his feet, wiping blood out of his eyes. "They're bloody animals," he said.

"They're bloody scared," Chris replied. "Like we all are."

"Thanks for getting me out of that."

"For a moment I thought you'd had it."

Meanwhile, the crowd had at last developed a conscience and was slowing down, some of them actually helping to pick up the fallen. But one man still lay on the ground and Jake didn't think he was breathing any more.

Jake had never realized how large the population of Shingleton was – or were they simply regenerating themselves, like the slime? He wondered if he was suffering from concussion. Hadn't that young man just run past him a few minutes ago? Surely that elderly woman had been helped by already?

Laura looked equally dazed and Chris was close to tears.

"What the hell are we going to do?" he said. "It's way out of control. We'll never get on a bus."

As he spoke they heard a shrill scream, followed by another and another. Then the smell came, less pungent than before, but horribly familiar.

"The slime," yelled Chris.

"Or the slimes," muttered Laura.

The slithering thing, about the size of a small pony, was sliding up the cobblestones, leaving a trail of dark blood, and Jake saw a deflated corpse enmeshed in its coils.

16

"It's hopeless," said Laura. "Completely hopeless."
The bus station was built into a hollow in the hill and flanked by a parade of shops on one side and a small factory on the other.

Half a dozen single-decker buses stood inside the garage and there were another two drawn up on the forecourt.

"They're completely overloaded," said Chris in despair.

Then another couple of buses crawled up the other side of the hill and drove empty into the garage which was surrounded by a ring of troops and police, trying to keep control. But every so often, would-be passengers managed to duck through the ring and tried to board.

Just to the side of the bus garage there were

large piles of sandbags behind which soldiers lay spreadeagled on the ground with high velocity rifles.

Helicopters whirred noisily overhead and there was an atmosphere of fearful anticipation.

"Aren't there any more?" yelled a woman at an inspector as he got off an empty bus while the troops tried to make passengers form a line.

"I've got two more coming back, but that's your lot for a while."

"Keep back," shouted one of the soldiers, raising his rifle at a group of young men who were pushing their way through to the front of the crowd. "Wait your turn!"

The inspector was waylaid by Jake. "How far are the buses going?" he asked.

"To Seaton."

"How long's the round trip taking?"

"About an hour. The drivers are having to crawl along because the vehicles are so overloaded. If only the army could make a better job of regulating the passengers coming on board, then we could turn the buses round much faster than we're doing now." He gazed at Jake. "You'd be better off running, fit young chap like you. Why don't—"

But his voice was drowned by more screaming from the edge of the crowd as a slime oozed round the corner by the parade of shops. The stuff stopped in its tracks and Jake saw with a jolt that it had developed a primitive head, rather like a slug, and its slimy body was harder, more rubbery.

The screaming died down and there was a terrible silence that was eventually broken by the starting up of the bus engines – and a renewed clamour to get on board.

The ring of troops raised their rifles and fired in the air as the crowd began to push past them, eventually succeeding in breaking the line and running towards the vehicles.

Some people fell and were immediately trampled and crushed. Jake grabbed Laura's arm, but she was wrenched away from him by the sheer force of the crowd. Horrified, he saw a burly man seize her round the waist, moving her on, shouldering his way to a bus, apparently determined to rescue someone who didn't want rescuing.

"Let me go!" Laura yelled. "You've got to let me go."

But the burly man still pushed her on. "I'm trying to help you, love," he shouted.

"I don't want help!"

As he pushed and she resisted, Laura hit her head on the side of the bus and went limp as he dragged her inside.

"Where is she?" yelled Chris. "Where's Laura?"

"She just caught a bus," said Jake.

Laura's head lay on a woman's shoulder as the bus sounded its horn, crawling through the crowd, and then making a sharp right-hand turn.

Chris and Jake began to run behind, beating at the windows, trying to attract Laura's attention.

"Watch out!" yelled someone.

Chris grabbed at Jake, pulling him back as a long tentacle of slime got between them and the bus.

The tentacle ran up one of the wheels in a haze of acid and a tyre burst in a mass of molten rubber. To make matters worse, the troops started firing but the bullets simply bounced off the rubbery texture of the slime's surface, making them rebound lethally into the crowd.

The bus lurched, skidded and gradually over-turned as if in slow motion. Attracted by the sound of shrieking metal, the slime oozed towards the wreckage, sending out more tentacles, while the bus began to sizzle, diesel pouring from its tank.

Jake and Chris hurled themselves into the smoking interior of the bus, fighting their way inside and grabbing Laura from what Jake was sure were a dead woman's arms. As they both dragged Laura out, acid fell from above, just missing them.

More passengers struggled out of the melting metal as Chris and Jake carried Laura through the crowd to a small yard at the back of the garage which had a couple of diesel pumps at the far end. It was hardly a safe place to be, but where *was* safe, wondered Jake.

Laura groaned and gradually came to, holding her head. "I hurt," she whispered.

"You've got a nasty bruise coming up," said Jake.

"You don't look so good yourself," Laura muttered while Chris glanced around fearfully, listening to the screaming, sure the slime was beginning to gorge itself. Then he saw a long thin tentacle ooze into the yard and over a dustbin which was soon reduced to an evil-smelling pool of plastic.

"For God's sake, move!" yelled Chris. "Can't you see what's heading towards us?"

Jake grabbed Laura's hand and they leapt the acidic stream, followed by Chris. As they raced for the far wall the tentacle turned, the smell over-powering, heading towards them with uncanny speed and accuracy.

"The slime knows where we are."

"It's instinct."

The tentacle paused and then shot forward as they backed up against the wall. This is it, thought Jake. Our luck's finally run out.

The tentacle fell a little short and then flailed, swiping the wall, recoiling and then swiping again. As it came in for the third time, Jake could feel the brickwork crumbling, shuddering violently and then collapsing, pitching them backwards in a cloud of dust.

They lay in the ruins, dazed and bruised, eventually scrambling to their feet. Looking back they could see the slime's tentacles waving and began to run up a steeply rising side street.

"Wait," gasped Laura.

An elderly woman was lying in the gutter, her face badly cut.

"We've got to get out," Chris yelled, but Laura was already kneeling beside the woman who was mouthing something that none of them could make out.

"We're here to help you," said Laura gently.

"My daughter—" she whispered.

"Where is she now?"

"Mary got swept away."

Laura helped the woman to her feet, and as she did so they saw a woman in a tracksuit staggering towards them, one arm hanging loosely by her side.

"Are you all right, Mum?"

"I got knocked over in the rush."

Jake glanced around. There was no one else in the side street but he could hear the revving of engines from the bus station. At any moment the slime could find them out. They couldn't afford to hang around.

"Where do you live?" asked Chris.

"Just down the road," said Mary. "I think we'll go back to the house."

"You can't do that." Laura was horrified. "They're trying to evacuate the town."

"And look at the mess they've made of it," said the elderly woman. "I'd rather stay in my own home. I'd rather die there than see people kicking each other to death, because that's all they're doing—"

"But the slime might get to you."

"I know," said Mary. "But there is such a thing as prayer. We both believe in God, and we'll put our trust in Him." She paused and then added, "We were both wondering if this stuff you call slime has come to destroy the human race for all the terrible things it's done."

"Armageddon," said Chris slowly.

"Why not?"

"I don't know—"

"We'll get home now." Mary sounded calm. "Now I've found Mum we'll stay together and wait and see what's in store for us. We'll be ready whatever happens. We'll be ready together."

Jake knew there was no point in trying to persuade them to escape.

As Mary and her mother began to walk back down the hill again, Jake shouted, "Good luck!"

Mary turned towards them with a sad smile. "It's not luck, is it? It's the wrath of God."

* * *

As they continued to climb the hill Chris said, "They're just a couple of cranks."

"I wonder." Laura was uneasy.

"So do I," said Jake. There had been such a quiet confidence in the two women's acceptance of their fate that he felt curiously disturbed.

17

Chris was shaking as they stood at the top of the hill. "Maybe they're right," he said. "Maybe it is Armageddon."

Stretched out below them in hazy afternoon sunshine were the marshes and the sea, the water glinting, distant and peaceful. There was hardly any wind.

On the hillside, however, dozens of slimes were crawling, leaving trails of cindery ash in the burnt grass behind them. Some were stationary while others were heading back towards the town.

"How did they get there?" whispered Laura.

"They must have oozed round the side of the headland. We're surrounded."

Just then an overloaded bus appeared, crawling

out on to the coast road towards Seaton. It was quickly followed by another, both vehicles moving so slowly that they couldn't have been doing more than ten miles an hour.

"They're going to get a nasty surprise," muttered Jake.

"Do you think the slime came round the headland to set up an ambush?" asked Chris.

"That would mean *real* intelligence," said Jake.

"You don't think they're being controlled?" wondered Laura.

"By God?" Chris was incredulous.

"By science," snapped Laura. "By some scientific programme."

"The research station's owned by the MOD," said Jake. "This is their responsibility."

"That's who we thought owned it." Laura paused. "But we haven't a clue who's really operating the place."

They continued to gaze down. The slimes were stationary now, most facing uphill, away from the road and the still slowly crawling buses.

"Maybe they're going to let the buses go," said Jake.

"I wouldn't bet on that." Chris was staring down at the beach where the coast road crossed a small bridge over a stream which ran out into the sea. "Do you see what I see?"

"What are you on about?"

"Focus your eyes on the part of the bridge that's nearest to the sea."

Laura and Jake gazed down.

"I still can't see anything," said Laura. "The sun's too bright."

Chris was staring down with enormous concentration. "There's something under the bridge. We've got to warn them."

Chris began to wave and shout, but as the vehicles slowly approached the bridge there was a sizzling sound and it suddenly melted into the stream. The first bus lurched, overturning on the beach, but the other bus braked and came to a shuddering halt.

For a while nothing happened.

Then the overturned bus burst into flames.

"There are more slimes going after the other bus," said Chris, but already the acid was eating into the bodywork and a tongue of flame belched from the diesel tank.

The passengers were pouring out, running over the pebbles, the young leaving the elderly behind, many of whom had already fallen.

Then the second bus exploded, the wreckage flying high in the air and raining down on the pebbles.

"We've got to do something for those people," yelled Laura. "We can't just stand here and watch them die."

"Yes, we can," said Chris. "There's nothing we *can* do." He spoke with a new authority.

"Chris is right," said Jake reluctantly. "We wouldn't stand a snowball's chance in hell."

Laura turned away from the blazing wreckage in despair.

Suddenly they heard the distant sound of a tannoy and saw a helicopter sweeping towards them, hovering over the blazing wreckage.

"Take cover. Take cover where you can. We appeal to all householders. Open up your homes. Take in as many people as you can. We repeat – take in as many people as you can. Then lock and bar your doors. Try to barricade your windows. We are attempting to deal with the debris of the chemical. I repeat, we are attempting to deal with the debris of the chemical—"

The message grew fainter as the helicopter veered away, back towards Shingleton.

"Let's go," said Chris.

"Where?" asked Jake.

"Anywhere. We'll find shelter and sit this out—"

"Wouldn't we be better off running for it?" demanded Jake.

"We'll never dodge the slime. They'll pick us off one by one. That's why they're here, isn't it?"

"They heard you," said Laura.

The slime were spreading out, as if responding to a challenge.

* * *

132

The streets were more crowded than ever, with fires raging out of control while a church was packed, noisy with prayer and the sound of weeping.

Someone was struggling to close the doors but was continually forced back as more and more people tried to push their way in. Others rattled on the front doors of houses and shops, piteously begging for refuge. But they were never opened. If there *are* people inside they're keeping very quiet, thought Jake. Doesn't *anyone* want to help, he wondered. Why were people being so selfish? He glanced at Laura and Chris as they strode down the street. A few hours ago, Shingleton had been home. Now it was a battlefield and he, Laura and Chris were warriors.

The sun beat down on bloodless deflated corpses lying in the streets, and from inside the blazing buildings they could hear the screams of the dying.

"We won't get any shelter here," said Laura. "Maybe we should go back to the harbour. I've got a key to the shop – if it's still there."

Just then an even larger crowd surged back from the marshes and they were once again swept into the seething mass as it plunged down the hill towards the harbour in a demented determination to survive.

For a moment Jake was wedged into the flailing mass, and when he looked round again he couldn't see either Chris or Laura. Where the hell had they got to?

Then Chris was beside him.

"Laura?" Jake yelled at him. "Where is she?"

"She must have run on down the hill."

"Why didn't you keep an eye on her?"

"Why didn't you?"

They glared at each other, fists clenched, wanting to fight but distracted by a sudden shout: "They're coming!"

The violence in Jake faded, replaced by a coil of cold fear, as if the slime itself had somehow got inside him, blubbery and twisting. He had lost all sense of direction and he and Chris gazed at each other helplessly.

"This way!" yelled Chris, and began to run down a narrow alley. Jake followed, terrified that he was going to lose him, that he would find himself alone in the streets.

The fact that Laura had slipped away from them and was at the mercy of the crowd obsessed him and he began to sob as he ran, wondering if Chris had any idea where he was going. Then he realized he must be heading towards the old fish market on the other side of the town.

Heavy iron gates topped with barbed wire were closed at the front of the abandoned market.

"We've got to get over somehow," yelled Chris.

"Isn't there another way in?"

"We haven't the time to find out."

With considerably difficulty they began to climb the gates, only finding the most precarious hand- and foot-holds. Several times Jake nearly fell, skinning his hands, sweat pouring off him in the heat, only wanting to find Laura but realizing at the same time that he would be of little use to her if he was eaten away by the toxic slime.

Chris reached the top of the gates first. Tearing off his T-shirt he laid the thin material across the barbed wire and painfully hauled himself across. With torn and bleeding hands, he eventually dropped to the ground.

Jake followed and half fell to the cobbles below.

"You OK?"

"Yes." He dragged himself to his feet, furious at looking so stupid and directing his anger at Chris. "What the hell are we doing here? I should be out looking for Laura."

"You won't be much use to her melted or sucked away, will you?" Chris said, echoing Jake's thoughts.

"We're just bloody cowards."

"Speak for yourself," snapped Chris, but that only inflamed Jake further.

"You panicked."

"You bet I did."

"What about Laura?"

"She'll be OK. She'll be back in the shop by now."

"Why the hell did you let her go?" Jake was beside himself with rage, determined to blame someone else for his mistake– and who better than Chris?

"Me? Let her go?" Chris was stung by the unfairness of it all. "It was you who did that."

"What did you say?"

"I said – it was you who let her go."

There was a momentary silence as Chris and Jake began to move towards each other in the cobbled yard, their eyes locked.

It was Jake who struck the first blow, but Chris ducked and Jake went wide. Despite his rage, he was amazed at what he was doing for he had never had a fight in his life. But now he wanted to go on hitting Chris until his face was a bloodied pulp. He had always hated Chris, and now Jake knew he had been given the opportunity to kill him.

Just as he swung again, Jake gazed over Chris's shoulder and then stood, transfixed.

"What is it?"

"Don't move."

"For God's sake—"

"It's just inside the door."

Chris turned to see that a small hole had been burnt into the wall that surrounded the yard.

The slime lay half-in and half-out of a partly eaten away metal door.

"How many more of them are here?" Chris was all too aware that if they had started to fight, one or even both of them could have ended up in the slime.

"Maybe just this one," muttered Jake.

"You always were too optimistic," Chris said viciously, but all the rage had drained out of Jake. Instead he stared at Chris with his torn clothes and scratched and bloodied face. The slime had turned them into animals.

Then Jake noticed something different. Why was the smell so faint? And wasn't there something odd about the slime? The thing looked shrunken and dried out.

Dried out?

"What's the matter with it?" They were both facing the slime now.

The sun was shining directly on to mottled flesh which moved slightly, making a dry, chafing sound.

Hope flared in Jake.

You always were too optimistic. Chris's scathing voice rang in his head. But there was definitely something very wrong with this piece of slime.

"It's dehydrating," said Jake. "The sun's drying it up."

"Is it dying?"

"I don't know." He tried to be cautious. "But whatever's happening, the thing's in a bad way. Surely even you can see that?"

Above them the sun continued to beat down from a cloudless sky, the heat fierce.

"Why didn't it make for the sea?"

Jake shrugged.

"Could they all be dying?"

"Depends on how many are taking the full glare of the sun. What about the slime that kept in the shade?" Then Jake had a sudden idea. "Wait a minute—"

"What is it?"

"Suppose the stuff could be diverted into the harbour? It'll be low tide soon and the sun'll be on the mud."

"Even better, if the gates to the dry dock were closed—" suggested Chris.

"They'd just burn through them."

"Not if they're still dehydrating. They'd be too feeble to move. Like this one."

Chris picked up a rusty iron stake from the yard and slowly approached the slime, his weapon held high. The stuff moved slightly as he stood over it, and gagged at the putrefying smell.

"What are you going to do?"

"I'm going to see what kind of shape it's in."

"Watch out for the acid."

"That *had* occurred to me," said Chris sarcastically. "I'm going to impale it. After all, it's a bloodsucker, isn't it?" He was nearer now, shaking slightly, his arm still raised, the stake poised.

"It could shoot stuff in your face," Jake warned him.

Chris stepped back a little and uneasily poked at the surface of the slime. "It's hard," he said. "I'm going to dig a bit deeper."

Chris poked harder with the stake, eventually penetrating the drying crust of the slime with a plopping sound. Dark blood and other less identifiable matter spurted up with a gurgling, rushing sound. The rancid smell got worse.

"Watch out for the acid," Jake repeated, really alarmed now. The sweat was pouring down his face and he felt sick.

"I don't think there *is* any acid," said Chris.

"Then what's all that?"

"Human blood and some kind of sticky stuff. It can't be toxic or this stake would have melted away. Wouldn't it?"

Jake came nearer, wanting to be reassured but still not sure. For a moment he felt a rising excitement, but when he thought of Laura the feeling faded. Suppose she was dead? Suppose Dad and Ben were dead, too?

Chris was still stirring at the filthy stuff curiously, but he suddenly turned to Jake as if he had been reading his thoughts. "What about my parents – what about yours? What about Laura?" Chris threw the stake into the grisly mound of slime. "You really go for her, don't you?"

"Yes," said Jake.

"So do I."

They stood beside the rotting slime, staring at each other intently.

"Let's have a truce," Chris said. "Until this is over."

"And then?"

"Every man for himself."

Suddenly a familiar voice cried out from behind the burnt away hole in the stone wall.

"What are you doing?"

It was Laura. Jake could hardly believe it as he ducked down and crawled through the hole, swiftly followed by Chris.

When Jake scrambled out, he looked up at Laura, amazed she was still alive. He'd never felt so full of joy.

"What were you doing in there?" she repeated.

"Just poking about in some slime," explained Chris.

"Where have you been?" demanded Jake. "I thought—"

"I got swept on by the crowd. I went into the church but there were too many people in there. I had to get out but I couldn't find you anywhere. Then I remembered the old market—" She paused. "Chris and I sometimes come here."

"You *what*?" Jake was shattered.

"Just to talk."

"To talk?" whispered Jake. Laura looked flustered and he knew she was lying. But he also knew they didn't have time for this – not if they wanted to survive.

"There was a piece of slime outside the church." Laura sounded shaky. "It was all dried up."

"So's this one," said Jake. "We should take a careful look round the streets and see how many more slime are getting dehydrated." He began to explain his hastily-improvised plan. Jake was careful to make the idea sound as if it had been his own and he could feel Chris's resentment.

"But what makes you think anyone's going to believe us?" Laura asked.

There was a strange stillness in the streets.

"What's happening?" Jake asked. "There doesn't seem to be anyone around."

"Everyone's found some kind of shelter at last," said Laura. "Except us."

"And the slime?" asked Chris.

"That doesn't seem much in evidence either."

"So it *is* dehydrating!" exclaimed Jake.

"I don't know," said Laura more cautiously now. "Let's get back to the harbour and see what's happening."

We're going in circles, thought Jake. That's all we're doing. Going in circles. And the slime's encircling *us*.

The silence felt suffocating as they began to walk down the steep streets, all of which bore the mark of the slime. Most of the fires had burnt themselves out and those that hadn't were gently smouldering.

Dodging the occasional piece of burning debris, they hurried on, keeping to the middle of the road.

There were no more dehydrated slimes, which was depressing, and the bloodless corpses that littered the streets were a barbaric sight. Pumped dry of blood, they looked like rag dolls. Did the slime have an ability just to suck the blood from the victims without melting them, Jake wondered? The slimes looked like blobs of nothing, but he suspected they were far more complex and sophisticated than he could ever have imagined.

Inside the buildings, Jake was conscious of a hidden throng, watching and waiting in dread. He could see shadowy figures, a face behind a window and someone twitching a net curtain. A child watched from the eaves of an attic and a girl suddenly emerged on a roof.

"What are you lot doing out on the streets?" she shouted, shattering the cottonwool silence.

"We're going to the harbour," Jake shouted back.

"Have you seen what's happening to the slime? The bits are all joining up."

"What do you mean?" demanded Laura fearfully.

"The thing's connecting together again."

Jake shuddered. What the hell was going on? "It's dying," he shouted. "It's dehydrated."

The girl shook her head. "We saw the slimes joining up to become a monster slime again."

So this is its last stand, thought Jake. Maybe by joining up the stuff can nourish itself better and fight off the dehydration.

"Where is it now?"

"The stuff slid past about five minutes ago. It's probably at the harbour by now."

Jake thought fast. "Does anyone know what's happened to the rescue services? To the army?"

"There have been helicopters buzzing about. Watching. My dad says they're going to drop bombs. That's why no one should be outside."

A man with a beard joined the girl on the roof. "Get off the streets! Are you crazy?" he shouted. "They're going to bomb the slime when it's re-connected."

"How do you know?" asked Laura.

"It's on the radio. Now get the hell off the streets! You haven't got time to ask questions."

"Can we come in with you then?" asked Chris desperately.

"You must be joking. We've got about forty people in this flat. We can't take any more."

"So where can we go?"

"I've no idea," the man bellowed at him.

"Let them in, Dad," his daughter urged him. "Three more can't make any difference."

"No way."

"Don't bother," said Chris. "We've already seen how uncaring people can be, so you're no surprise!"

"If the slime's joined up the thing's going to make an easier target," Laura said, looking worried. "They're bound to have another go at it."

"They must be crazy. However much they decimate the stuff, each tiny piece will have a new life of its own. Haven't they got the message yet?" Jake was furious.

Suddenly he saw a familiar vehicle parked up a side street – a Jaguar with blacked-out windows.

"What's happening?" said Laura as Jake came to an abrupt halt.

"That's Millard's car. I'm going to talk to him."

"Don't be long," said Chris.

"Anything could happen," said Laura. "And it's not just the slime we've got to worry about. It's the bombs, too." She sounded anxious and for a minute Jake wavered.

"I shan't be long," he said, pounding towards the Jaguar, once again thinking of Chris and Laura alone together in the abandoned market.

Jake wrenched open the back door only to find Millard, unscathed and still smartly dressed, sitting on the back seat, a bundle of papers on his lap. Beside him was Ben.

Jake was incredulous, his heart hammering painfully, the shockwaves making him dizzy.

"What the hell are you doing here? And where's Dad?"

Ben looked up at him in confusion, while Millard merely said, "Why aren't you taking cover?"

"Because I don't choose to."

"The chemical's going to be bombed."

Jake could see that one of Millard's papers was headed EFFLUENT CONTROL.

"Why are *you* here, Ben?" Jake felt as if the world he had known had suddenly become completely distorted in a way he couldn't possibly be expected to understand.

Millard intervened. "Your uncle was wandering the streets – like you. I picked him up. It was George's idea." He leant towards the driver. "Wasn't it?"

"Yes, sir. He wouldn't have stood a chance. The slime was only a minute away."

"So why didn't you help other people, too?" demanded Jake.

"They'd got under cover, hadn't they?" Millard replied.

Jake turned back to his uncle. "Dad went off with the Knights, but he was looking for you everywhere."

"We met up at the jetty. They should be on board the *Lucky Strike* by now."

"So why did you come back?"

"To find you, of course. Your father should never have left you behind. I've been looking for you ever since. You lot have been grossly irresponsible. This isn't a game – as you've probably found out."

Jake paused. Ben sounded all too plausible. "We've got this idea."

"I haven't got time for your ideas," snapped Millard.

"If the slime can be got into the dry dock, the stuff might dry out in the sun. That's what's happened to some of the slime when it got dispersed."

"Certainly the substance has weakened," said Millard dismissively. "As I expected – and once it's been bombed that'll be it."

"It'll separate again. Even a shred will have life."

"Not in its weakened state," snapped Millard.

"I think you're wrong."

"And I don't think you can expect me to take you seriously. As your uncle said – you've surely discovered this isn't a game."

Jake hit the side of the door with his fist in fury.

"Get under cover." Millard gazed at him contemptuously while Ben looked away.

The driver started the engine.

"Where are you taking my uncle?"

"There's help needed at one of the first aid posts we're setting up."

"Why can't *we* help?"

"Because we need responsible adults."

As the Jaguar began to glide away, Jake hit the passenger door again, just as Ben was shouting, "Find some cover – and then get to the boat."

Jake watched the Jaguar disappear round the corner, hurt and surprise spreading inside him. His uncle loved him, so why had he just abandoned him on the streets?

When Jake rejoined Chris and Laura he decided not to tell them, for the moment at least, about the surprise meeting with his uncle. He wanted to think it all through. Then he realized they were standing still, staring ahead.

"I don't believe this," gasped Chris.

The reassembled slime was enormous and moving slowly. Jake glanced down at his watch. It was just after four and the hard, bright sunlight showed no sign of lessening. Keep shining, prayed Jake. *Please* keep shining. But as he gazed up at the sky he saw clouds on the horizon. Some of them were dark.

"Don't let it rain," said Laura aloud. "Please, don't let it rain."

The slime was making a dry rumbling sound and they dodged into an alley, flattening themselves against the wall, hearing the stuff slow down.

"It's scented us," gasped Laura.

They began to back off down the alley but the slime had come to a scraping halt, poking its blunted, sightless head round the corner, making a kind of rasping sound.

They froze, surprised there was no tentacle, no bubbling, scorching acid.

"It's in trouble," said Chris.

The slime was pock-marked and there was an over-powering smell of corruption, its surface a dry crust.

"Severe case of sunburn," muttered Jake.

"I can smell something else," said Laura suddenly. "Isn't that chlorine?"

"The leisure centre," Chris whispered.

"It's only a couple of streets away," said Jake. "Maybe the slime's not scenting us after all. It's the pool."

Slowly the slime withdrew and began to slide down the main street again, its body crackling and flaking.

"The slime could rehydrate in the pool." Laura came to the same conclusion as Jake and Chris.

"The thing's too big to get in." Chris was trying to keep calm.

"I think you've forgotten something. The slime's flexible; it can curl up, all cosy like."

"We've got to get the pool drained," Laura yelled at them.

"There's something else," said Jake as they broke into a run. "The leisure centre's going to be full of people taking shelter. We've got to get the building evacuated. Fast!"

The glass doors were locked, and gazing inside Jake could see that the whole of the large foyer was jam-packed with people. Some were sitting on the floor, others asleep.

He rapped at the glass on which was emblazoned the centre's logo and name: UTOPIA.

"The slime's on its way," yelled Laura, crashing with her fists.

Few people looked up and those that did hurriedly looked away again. It was as if Jake, Laura and Chris were invisible as they continued to bang at the doors.

In the end a man staggered to his feet, walked slowly over and gestured at them to go away.

"The slime!" Laura screamed at him through the glass. "It'll be here in a few minutes."

He shrugged, seemingly unable to hear, and was walking away again when she hit her head against the glass in a last desperate attempt to communicate.

She staggered back as Jake wrenched at her arm, determined not to let her do it again. "For God's sake—"

"He's coming back," said Chris.

The man was tall with a pair of half-rimmed glasses, and looked concerned as he unlocked one of the doors.

"What did you do that for?" He was bewildered, too. "You some kind of nutter?"

"The slime's coming," said Jake. "It's joined together again."

"*What?*"

"The segments – they've all joined up."

"Ridiculous!"

"It's true—"

"You've got to get out," gasped Chris.

"No way."

"The slime needs water. It's dehydrating."

"So there's some hope—" He was beginning to believe them.

"Not if it gets in here. If the slime can reach the pool there's a chance it *could* rehydrate."

The man's lip curled as if he had to dismiss what they were saying, not prepared to face the reality of the new threat. "So this is your idea of a joke, is it?"

Jake gazed at him uncomprehendingly.

"Do you realize how many hundreds have died in this catastrophe? Why are you stupid enough to wind people up? Typical of today's youth, aren't you? No respect. No sensitivity. Nothing. Well, you're not coming in here."

"That's exactly what I am doing," said Jake, shoving him in the chest. The man, caught off-balance, fell back into the crowded foyer.

"Now you've done it," said Chris, as he and Laura followed Jake inside.

Although he was unsure of himself, Jake began to shout: "Listen, everybody! The slime's on its way."

But Jake was already too late as the glass door shattered and the blind, blunt head of the dehydrating slime appeared, making a desperate hissing sound.

* * *

The slime had degenerated. There were ragged cuts and abrasions at its joins which were weeping a thick substance that had no acidic haze. Most of its body was covered in a blackened and flaking crust. Jake saw a huge piece of rot fall, dark and bloodied, on the floor of the foyer.

The man with the glasses stared ahead, his mouth opening and shutting but no words coming out.

The occupants of the leisure centre cowered back, not daring to move.

The slime seemed to hesitate.

Then, slowly and painfully, as if its senses were impaired, the thing headed for another set of glass doors, smashing through them and dragging the rest of its crusted body across the floor.

People began to make a path, their panic receding, realizing if they let the blackened thing through they wouldn't be harmed.

The spectator seats that were banked up on either side of the pool were already packed with refugees.

Once again the slime hesitated, as if its faculties were no longer functioning properly. The blunted head seemed to sniff the chlorine-scented air as with a final effort it slid through the debris of the doors, up on to the poolside and entered the shallow end with what sounded like a sigh.

Jake reckoned that the creature's reconstituted body must be at least fifty metres long.

The slime continued on into the deep end, a

huge wave rising and splashing over the edge, soaking some of the crowd. Then the slime continued to drag itself along, coil after coil, until its heaving blackened body completely filled the pool.

The crowd was silent. A few bubbles were escaping from under the slime's crust, making a slight plopping sound.

"*Is* it dead?" whispered Chris.

"I don't know," replied Jake. "It's like the slime's just resting."

"And disintegrating. Look," hissed Laura, and they craned forward to see that shards of dead skin were beginning to float up from the bottom of the pool, lying on the surface like dark wood shavings.

Then there was a slopping sound and a much more substantial piece of rot floated up.

Tentatively, Jake, Chris and Laura went over for a closer look but when they arrived at the shallow end Jake whispered, "It *is* regenerating."

The blistered crust was still breaking away and floating to the surface with a soft, sighing sound. But a tentacle was beginning to move – and then another.

"You have to get out," yelled Laura at the crowd. "The slime's going to go toxic again."

Laura couldn't work out whether the people in the spectator seats disbelieved her or were simply too terrified to move.

Then a young couple got up and tiptoed down the

steps towards the pool, treading cautiously past the slime and through the shattered doors to the foyer.

Others began to follow, eyes on the monstrously regenerating coils and the floating scales of dead skin. Soon more came, no longer attempting caution, hurrying down the steps, pushing and shoving, desperate to get out.

A strong smell of sulphur filled the air and acidic steam began to rise from the pool as the coils, slowly, very slowly, began to move.

Terrified, the crowd broke into a run and a large man in a football shirt and jeans began to punch at someone who was trying to get past him. For a moment they locked together, arms around each other's waists. Then they overbalanced and rolled into the scummy surface of the pool.

They both began to cleave the water in a fast crawl, arms and legs thrashing, but the slime was close behind, a dense cloud of foul-smelling acidic steam belching out.

The two men screamed and screamed again as their flesh began to peel down to the bone. Soon all that was left floating on the surface was a half-melted trainer.

"Let's go," said Chris as the blunted head rose from the boiling water, but the crowd in the foyer was too great, closely packed and struggling against each other in a hopeless mass.

"We'll go the other way," yelled Jake. "Down

through the squash courts." Followed by Chris and Laura, he turned, running alongside the pool, past the writhing coils, towards the stairs. Then he realized how selfish they were being and Jake turned round. "There's a way out," he shouted to the crowd. "Follow us."

19

Now they were tearing down a passage that led past the squash courts towards a sign that read EMERGENCY EXIT, followed by a steady stream of survivors. Above the gasping of their breathing Jake could hear a steady dripping sound. Suddenly he smelt sulphur and saw droplets burning through the ceiling.

"Watch out!" he yelled. "There's acid coming through. Keep to the sides and run like hell!"

Pounding down the corridor they finally reached the emergency exit, but he could hear behind them the screams of those who had not been so lucky, who were feeling the full force of the acid. Horrified, Jake realized he had unintentionally led the survivors into a trap – and they were survivors no more.

Jake kicked at the bar, the door swung open and with a sense of glorious relief they found themselves in the car park outside.

For a moment the three friends paused, out of breath and completely exhausted. Then Chris yelled, "Look at that wall – it's bulging."

He's right, thought Jake. It was only a small bulge but he could see the concrete was already cracking and water was spurting out. Then a helicopter came into view, buzzing above the empty streets and hovering over the leisure centre whose concrete walls were now disintegrating.

Jake waved desperately and the helicopter seemed to hesitate for a moment before diving down towards them. As it landed in the car park, the navigator gave amplified instructions.

"Run under the blades. Watch your heads. Do it now."

The noise was deafening but they didn't hesitate, charging head-down towards the open door and clambering inside. As the helicopter rose into the air, a huge torrent of water spurted into the car park, carrying with it a mass of debris, dozens of human bodies and the huge coils of the slime, the acid destroying everything in its path.

The helicopter continued to climb and the navigator who had helped them inside asked, "What the hell happened?"

"The slime's regenerated," said Chris as they veered away from the writhing coils and headed towards the harbour.

"We've got to talk to someone in authority," Laura said, seeing Jake glance at his watch. It was just coming up to six o'clock and the sun was beginning to lose its heat.

He gazed down for a final glimpse of the slime only to see the thing was beginning to move faster now, squirming down a side street, acid rising in a cloud of steam.

"See who?" asked the navigator doubtfully.

"Whoever's in charge," said Jake.

"That'll be Commander Denver."

"Police?"

"Royal Marines."

"So he's taking all the decisions then?" asked Chris.

"That's right."

"We need to see him," said Jake.

"What about?"

"We know how to kill the slime."

The navigator gazed at them and then shouted to the pilot. "No problem then," he said. "Chemical disaster over. Kids to the rescue." He grinned at them patronizingly.

"We mean it," said Laura angrily. "Why won't you believe us?"

"Because it seems unlikely a pack of kids would have the answer."

Jake lost his temper. "Why don't you bloody listen? We want to speak to Commander Denver."

"Top secret, eh?" The navigator was openly laughing at them.

They were flying low over the shattered harbour. The navigator moved over to the pilot and muttered in his ear. When he'd finished they both laughed.

"Can you contact Denver now?" persisted Jake. "Tell him we'd like to talk to him right away."

"He's a busy man."

"I promise you we've got a solution," said Laura. She paused and then added, "We broke into Craven Marsh research station. We *know* what to do."

"To do what?"

"Control the slime."

The navigator paused and stopped grinning. Then he spoke to the pilot who pressed the radio control and spoke into his microphone.

The navigator turned back. "All right. But if you're having us on in a crisis like this – you're going to be in big trouble."

"There couldn't *be* bigger trouble than this," said Jake, gazing down at the charred and twisted devastation that had once been Shingleton harbour.

Commander Denver's headquarters were based in a camouflage-painted caravan which was parked amongst the burnt-out vehicles and sheds on the quayside.

The harbour area had been sealed off with police tape, sandbags and barriers that read EMERGENCY. STRICTLY NO ADMITTANCE.

A large number of military personnel in trucks and armoured vehicles were present while a couple of tanks had just arrived. There was also a considerable police presence, with dozens of squad cars and motorcycles, and some TV camera teams had been penned in a compound near the burnt-out garage.

An atmosphere of uneasy expectation was growing as what looked like a massive flame thrower with a huge barrel was being pulled into position by a group of soldiers with walkie-talkies.

The helicopter landed on an improvised pad alongside three others and the navigator escorted Jake, Laura and Chris to the caravan. There he handed them over to a soldier who took them to a reception area where a senior officer sat behind a desk. He ushered them into the back of the caravan which was banked with computers, on which the slime could be seen heading slowly down the deserted streets of the town.

Commander Denver was young, tall and thin, with a small moustache, and was wearing an immaculate uniform. He looked harassed, and glanced at them impatiently.

"I gather you have some information from Craven Marsh. Please be brief."

"We broke into the research station and saw the slime escape."

There was a pause.

"How did you get in there?" demanded Denver.

Laura began to explain what had happened, but he hardly seemed to be listening, continually turning to look at the screens and the half-dozen men at the computers.

"We think we've found a way of killing the thing," Laura continued.

Denver raised his eyebrows. "Really?" he asked.

"The tide's out," said Jake. "So this is the ideal time."

"To do what?"

"The stuff rehydrated in the pool and we know it's not just a chemical substance. The slime has an instinct. It needs water."

Denver cleared his throat. "Get to the point."

Jake stared at him with momentary uncertainty. "If you can trap the slime in the dry dock, there's a chance of the sun drying the thing out again."

Denver got to his feet. "So that's it?"

They stared at him.

"I'd thought there was an outside chance you might have picked up some information at Craven Marsh that could be of use to us. Instead you're just three kids with a crazy idea."

"So what are *you* going to do?" interrupted Laura as Jake shrugged. He should have realized there was no way of communicating with these people.

"We have a device that will destroy the chemical immediately."

"You mean you're going to bomb it," said Chris scornfully.

"We don't intend to do anything of the kind. The device we have in position now will drench the chemical with a special preparation which will dissolve it completely." He paused and looked at his watch. "I'm going to have you escorted out of the harbour area and I suggest you try to take immediate cover." Then Denver softened slightly and became patronizing. "I know you've been trying to do your best. You've behaved bravely – all three of you. As soon as we've got rid of the chemical we'll get you medical help. But for the moment you've got to take cover."

"Where did you get your preparation?" asked Jake.

"From Craven Marsh."

"What happens if it doesn't work?"

"There's no question of that." Denver turned to one of his officers. "Lieutenant Lawrence, will you show our young friends out? Take them over to Cobbs House."

Jake knew this was a building that had once been the Harbour Master's house and was now a fishing museum.

"Please take my advice and wait there until the emergency is over."

"Who else have you got in there?" demanded Laura.

"The mayor. The head of local social services, some of the town council – and now you." Commander Denver smiled at them. "So consider yourselves lucky – you're part of the privileged few. You've become VIPs, so try to behave accordingly." Then he became serious again. "You must appreciate we have a huge death toll here, and we don't want it growing bigger."

"We were trying to help," muttered Chris, furious at being so crudely marginalized.

"Let's go," said Lieutenant Lawrence. He was short, running to fat and avuncular. "You need a place of safety as much as anyone else."

"What are you going to do then?" asked Laura furiously. "Tuck us up in bed with a nice milky drink?"

The sun was sinking into the sea in a bright orange glow that turned the surface into a shimmering mass of colour.

"Don't even think about trying to leave," Lieutenant Lawrence had warned them as he departed, locking the front door of Cobbs House behind him.

Now, stuck in a small, dark room on the ground

floor, Jake, Laura and Chris became increasingly depressed.

Unable to bear the inactivity, Jake went out into the hall and tried the handle of the front door for the third time, but it wouldn't budge. He paced restlessly around the main room, which was full of display stands and rather dusty-looking glass cases, hearing a buzz of conversation from the other occupants of Cobbs House somewhere upstairs.

He was beginning to feel quite frantic, torn between worrying about his father and his strange encounter with Ben and the deep frustration he was feeling about the way they had been rejected. Then Jake cursed himself for his selfishness. He hurried back to the little room, wanting to reassure Laura, but when he went in Jake saw that she was in Chris's arms.

"What the hell do you think you're doing?" he shouted aggressively. "Leave her alone."

"Why don't you get lost!" snapped Chris. "Laura's been through a hell of a lot and—"

"So have we all."

"She's not your property, you know," said Chris belligerently. "You don't own her."

Jake completely lost control, punching him hard in the face and then throwing him back against the wall. Chris's head cracked against the hard stone-work and he slid limply to the floor, blood running from his nose.

"For God's sake!" yelled Laura.

"I don't like him touching you."

"Don't *I* have a say in that? As Chris said, you don't own me. No one owns me." She was kneeling down, trying to stem the blood with a filthy handkerchief.

"I'm sorry." Jake felt slightly faint, amazed at what he'd done, hopeless exhaustion sweeping through him.

"That isn't enough." Laura glared at him. "You really are pathetic, aren't you?"

Chris was coming to now, bewildered and in pain. "What happened?"

"Jake happened." She mopped again at the blood pouring from Chris's nose.

"I've said I'm sorry. I just don't like—"

"Chris touching me. Well, if you really want to know, I *wanted* him to touch me. I was thinking about my family, wondering if they'd be wiped out and—" Laura was partly angry, partly close to tears.

"Look," said Jake desperately. "I've said I'm sorry. I don't know what happened. I just lost it for a moment. Chris – I feel really bad about this. I didn't know what I was doing."

As Chris staggered shakily to his feet, the door opened and Ben stood on the threshold.

His uncle strode over to Jake and grabbed him by

the shoulders, ignoring the bloodied Chris. "Thank God you're safe."

"I thought Millard was going to drop you off at the first aid post."

"This *is* the first aid post – or will be."

"What about Dad?" said Jake accusingly. "He must be worried sick about you."

Ben frowned. "Aren't you going to introduce me to your mates?"

"You know Laura, and this is Chris." Introductions seemed more than inappropriate and neither of them replied.

Jake still felt deeply ashamed. Had he blown it with Laura for ever? The idea seemed even worse than a slime attack.

"I've been shacked up with the mayor and the town council and social services. You'd better fill me in on what's been happening outside."

Jake looked at Laura, but she turned away. "All right," he said. "I'll fill you in."

"I don't know what the hell's going to happen," said Ben when Jake had finished. "As you say, Craven Marsh have concocted the stuff in that device on the harbour. Let's hope it works, that's all." Ben seemed much more confident than he had been when Jake saw him in the back of Millard's Jaguar. "If Craven Marsh flunk it again, then the last recourse we have is the navy."

A siren began to wail outside and Ben hurried to

the front door, fumbling in his pocket and to Jake's surprise bringing out a key.

The slime was blackened but only in patches, and although it was weak the acid haze still hung like an aura.

As the stuff slid down the length of the quayside several cars and a personnel carrier burst into flame.

The barrel of the device on the quayside swivelled and fired a black chemical substance, searing the surface of the slime. But almost immediately the substance rebounded, smothering the barrel.

There was a massive explosion and red-hot metal fell on to the square, twisted and partly melted, while two bodies lay in the debris.

Shivering slightly, as if suffering from shock, the slime began to ooze back over the ruins of the harbour wall and across the dried-out mud towards the sea.

Jake watched it go, unable to believe that the much-vaunted weapon could have failed so badly. Chemical against chemical – and the toxic slime had won yet again.

For a moment Jake wondered if someone at Craven Marsh had deliberately produced the wrong formula so that the *real* weapon could get away unscathed. Could there be a conspiracy, he speculated. He couldn't take his eyes away from the two bodies. What had they died for? A government conspiracy to manufacture a secret compound that could decimate millions?

"So much for Commander Denver's grand plan," said Laura. "And so much for Craven Marsh's antidote. Over in seconds."

Gradually, the survivors emerged from the houses and shops and pubs, blinking in the late-afternoon light. They stood behind the barriers surrounding the harbour in their hundreds, silently watching the slime ooze over the rocks towards the tideline.

"The sea will just regenerate the bloody thing," said Chris.

The army, police and rescue services were gazing at the slime silently and intently. Few of them spoke. Then a helicopter rose from its pad and began to follow the blackened chemical monster.

"How about Plan B," said Ben. "The good old Royal Navy." It was impossible to tell how he was feeling.

"Let's hope that doesn't happen until the slime's well clear of the harbour," said Jake. He could see a couple of destroyers cautiously standing off.

"But suppose the slime *doesn't* go out to sea?" wondered Laura. "Suppose the thing hugs the shore and makes another landing when it's rehydrated? Another town could be destroyed, or it might come back to have another go at Shingleton."

"Keep looking on the bright side," muttered Ben.

"The slime is heading out to sea," said Chris.

In the twilight they all had difficulty making out its course, but a couple of helicopters were buzzing over the wallowing bulk and in their searchlights Jake could see that Chris was right.

Jake looked around at the hundreds of weary and dazed-looking men, women and children on the quayside, dirty and dishevelled, cut and bruised.

Dozens of troops stood in front of the crowd, surveying the shattered debris, watching the slime gather speed, no doubt slowly reviving as it swam out to sea.

"Are you thinking what I'm thinking?" muttered Chris.

"The slime's going to attack the destroyers," said Jake. "And that means we were wrong."

"What about?"

"We thought the stuff only had an instinct. Now I reckon the slime's got intelligence. It can think for itself."

The crowd grew silent as the slime neared the ship, moving faster than ever as the sky darkened. But to Jake it was as if the whole world was darkening. What *was* the slime? For what purpose had it really been made?

A wind rose, making the waves slap at the shore. Searchlights weaved about on the swell and there was shouting from the crowd as they realized what was going to happen.

"I don't like this," said Ben. "I don't like this one little bit."

The destroyer seemed to shudder, and in the arc of the searchlights Jake saw the pale blunted head of the slime make contact with the starboard bow. A flame licked along the decks, steel went into meltdown and there was the dull thump of an explosion, a whole sheet of flame now lighting the sky with a jaundiced and unearthly glow.

The destroyer upended and went down stern first, making a grinding sound. The terrible noise went on until she had completely disappeared, leaving only a spreading slick of oil.

People in the crowd began to weep and others swore. Never had Jake felt so helpless.

In the light of the helicopter, the toxic slime floated on the waves, seeming to watch the small items of wreckage as they bubbled to the surface, as if satisfied by its work of destruction. Then the tide began to draw it back towards the harbour.

"That's it then," said Ben. "We'll get to the *Lucky Strike*. We'll have to move fast. Your dad will think you're dead – that we're all dead."

But Jake was determined to make one last stand. "We'll call up Charlie Mason, the harbour master, and try to convince him that the last chance we have is to let the slime drift back into the harbour – and then into the dry dock."

"How *can* we convince him?" demanded Laura

as they began to push their way back through the numbed crowd.

"I know the guy," said Jake. "I've known him all my life."

"That doesn't mean he's going to listen to you," said Ben, and Jake felt an impending sense of failure.

Surprisingly, however, Chris was supportive. "It was different before," he said. "The authorities had plans – plans they were sure were going to work. But now they've got to realize the slime's got powers they never dreamed of and there's nothing they can do but take the risk we're all suggesting to them. It could just work!"

The seaweed and barnacle-hung jetty jutted out from a thin strip of sandy beach and moored alongside was the *Lucky Strike*, dimly lit, bobbing up and down, the wind in her rigging making a slight whistling sound.

Exhausted and apprehensive, Jake, Laura, Chris and Ben clambered aboard.

"Who's that?" shouted Dan Oakley, coming out on deck with a torch.

"It's me, Dad."

"Jake?"

"And Ben – and everyone else. We're safe."

Dan was so overjoyed to see his son that his eyes filled with tears and he clasped Jake fiercely and protectively. "Thank God."

"Where are my parents?" demanded Laura.

"They decided to go on down to Seaton to reassure your grandmother," said Dan. "All the phone lines are down." He turned to Chris. "But the Knights used their mobile and told me to tell you they'd given your folks a lift. Their car had run out of petrol."

Chris gave a wild cry of joy and Laura kissed him. Then they hugged each other while Jake felt a surge of despair.

"Do you know what's been going on, Dad?"

"You bet I do. I've been up and down the coast to see the damage for myself. Shingleton's just a smoking ruin – and I've been keeping in radio contact with the rest of the fishing fleet. That slime thing's still wallowing about out there."

"Are there any survivors from the destroyer?"

"Precious few."

"So what's going to happen?"

"The other ship's pulled back. Maybe they're going to observe the thing during the night and try a missile from a greater distance sometime tomorrow morning."

Another reason for delay, Jake thought miserably. More time for the slime to fully regenerate. And as for the missile – it would only shred the thing to grow again and again.

"The slime moved incredibly fast," said Chris.

"The filthy stuff headed for that destroyer like there was no tomorrow."

Jake began to tell his father about their plan to trap the slime in the dry dock. "It's getting carried towards the harbour now and we could be in with a chance. Can *you* speak to Charlie Mason? I just don't think he's going to listen to me. No one else does," he said, with a rush of self-pity.

But Dan seemed equally defeated. "Even if we did convince Charlie, he can't go it alone. He'd need authorization."

"For Christ's sake, Dad – we've *got* to do something."

"Why can't *you* speak to Charlie, Jake?" insisted Laura.

"I told you – he won't listen to me," replied Jake frankly.

"Give it a swing," urged Chris.

"The army will never agree to trap the slime so near the town," snapped Ben dismissively. "Why waste your energy?"

"The slime's as exhausted as we are. The thing could stay dormant until dawn. Give Charlie a go," Chris urged him.

Jake felt sudden resolution. He needed to get his confidence back. "OK. I'll give it a swing then."

"Do bear in mind you're wasting everyone's time," yelled Ben, but Dan began to dial up Charlie Mason and he turned away.

"Harbour Master."

"It's Dan. I've got Jake here. He wants a word."

"He's safe? Put him on."

Jake was nervous and glanced at Laura and Chris.

"Go for it," said Laura. "Convince him."

Jake felt as if he would be quite unable to convince anyone of anything ever again. "Hi, Charlie," he said uneasily.

"You're all right, then?"

Jake plunged in, feeling stupid and inadequate. "I had this idea."

"What idea?"

"The tide's floating the slime in towards the harbour."

"I've already warned Commander Denver."

"What's he going to do?" Jake was encouraged. At least Charlie Mason hadn't dismissed him out of hand.

"I don't know."

Jake took a deep breath. He had to pitch the idea now – and pitch it as purposefully as he could. "Why don't you let the stuff drift back into the harbour? Then you could open the gates to the dry dock. The tide might take the slime into the dock and, if the gates are closed again, the thing might dry out during the night. When the morning sun gets up it might finish the job."

"You use the word 'might' rather a lot, don't you, Jake?" Charlie sounded as if he was trying to be patient, trying not to lose his temper. "Why don't you get some sleep? The authorities are working on the problem. I've still got faith in them."

Jake knew that what had seemed like a good start had turned into even more rejection. Why had he been stupid enough to try and sell the idea to Charlie, a sceptical man at the best of times?

Then to Jake's surprise, his father suddenly grabbed the phone. "Sorry, Charlie, but I think my boy's got a point."

"For God's sake, Dan—" Ben tried to intervene while Charlie Mason seemed at a complete loss for words.

"Let the filth float back into the harbour and trap it in the dry dock."

"It'll attack the town again."

"Not if it's exhausted. Jake's right. The more the slime's immersed in water, the more it can regenerate. The stuff's used up its energy right now. But it won't be like that for long unless it's kept out of the sea."

There was silence.

Then Charlie said, "I can't take the responsibility on my own. I could lose my job. I'll have to check with Denver. I'll call you back." There was another long pause. Then he added with sudden honesty, "The trouble is, Denver hasn't contacted me for hours. I don't know what the hell he's doing. I've got this feeling we're *all* being kept in the dark."

"Thanks, Dad," said Jake when his father had put down the phone. "I appreciate that."

"We *all* appreciate that," put in Laura.

Dan shrugged. "It may not do any good. Charlie's running scared, like we all are – and he's got no authority in this crisis. No authority at all. And as for this Denver, I don't like the cut of his gybe."

Jake grasped his father's arm. He had never loved him so much.

"I think we should take a look at this wallowing mess for ourselves," said Dan as they sat in the cabin below the wheelhouse, waiting for Charlie Mason to call them back.

"We don't want to bump into a heap of floating slime," said Ben.

"It would be a wipe out," said Jake grimly. "But we *won't* bump into the slime, will we, Dad?"

"We'll certainly keep our distance."

"Suppose the stuff wakes up and goes for us?" Chris seemed to have been infected by Ben's negativity.

"You're right." Ben looked pleased that Chris had faltered.

"Is he?" Laura frowned. "We can't just sit here and do nothing. We need to know what kind of shape the slime's in."

The phone rang and Dan grabbed the receiver. "Oakley." He pressed the loudspeaker so that everyone could hear what Charlie was saying.

"I've spoken to Denver. Predictably enough, he's against the idea. He says there's too much danger to the town."

Dan swore. "Did you tell them where the idea came from?"

"No. I took responsibility for the initiative. I did my best, but he just refused to listen. He said the slime was badly weakened – and that it would be taken out to sea on the next tide. Then he was going to attack the thing with missiles."

"Doesn't he realize that even if he blows the stuff into the most minute particles, there's a chance of each and every one regenerating? Why doesn't he learn from experience?"

Charlie didn't reply directly and only said, "You know there's been this fault on the dry dock gates?"

There was a hint of cunning in Charlie's voice and Jake suddenly wondered if another conspiracy was about to be hatched – a conspiracy that might, just might, be rather useful. He felt a flicker of renewed hope.

"I've had them checked a couple of times, but they keep malfunctioning."

"In what way?" asked Dan, with increasing curiosity.

"When the tide goes out and the water recedes, the gates occasionally jam shut. This could be one of those – unfortunate – times."

"You old devil! So Jake *has* convinced you."

"I should have been convinced much more quickly. This situation's being mishandled – maybe deliberately. But I haven't got time for self-recrimination. I'm prepared to take a risk, and I gather the town's finally being evacuated. So if the slime does attack, the casualty rate might be a little more limited."

"You've had a sudden change of heart, Charlie."

"Call it the dripping tap process. You know me, Dan, I have to be convinced. Tell Jake he did that and I'm grateful to him."

"Well done, Jake," said Laura, and even Chris clapped him on the back.

For the first time in a long time Jake not only felt appreciated but had a sense of his own value.

"We'll wait for an hour," said Dan. "And then check out our slimy friend."

"You're not thinking of prodding the slime in the right direction, are you?" said Ben. "What would you like me to do? Give the stuff a poke with a boat-hook?"

"Hopefully the slime will drift in of its own accord and then it's up to Charlie," said Dan.

"So why put ourselves in danger?" asked Chris. He seemed to have lost his nerve.

"I think we should stand by," said Dan quietly. "If the gates *are* faulty, then we can't rely on them."

"So it *is* a boat-hook job," said Ben with a grin.

Jake glanced at Laura. "I'd like to see this through. But no one *has* to come."

"I'm with you," she said.

"What about you, Chris?" asked Jake.

"I've always wanted to fight the slime," he said with studied nonchalance. "Looks like I've got my chance at last."

While Chris helped Ben to brew up some cocoa in the galley and Dan checked the wheelhouse, Jake and Laura were left alone in the cabin.

"I'm sorry I hit Chris," Jake said uneasily, wondering how angry she still was with him.

"I'm sorry, too – for your sake. You shouldn't be so possessive."

"But I am," he muttered.

"Of everybody?"

"Of you."

"I don't like being a possession." Laura was staring at him thoughtfully, and it was impossible to know what she was thinking.

"I'm sorry," he apologized again, but rather more reluctantly. Why did she always put him in the wrong? "Fancy a beer?" he asked eventually.

"OK."

"I'll get us all one." Forgetting that Ben and Chris were making cocoa, Jake went over to the fridge, but found it empty. "Maybe there's some in here." He went over to the cold box under the table and pulled it out. "That's odd."

"What is?" asked Laura distantly.

"Why padlock the cold box?"

"How should *I* know?"

Jake went over to the pegs where his father kept the keys, but couldn't find one that would open the padlock. As he searched, he could hear Ben talking to Chris in the galley. He seemed to be in the middle of telling him a very involved story about a yacht he had once owned.

Jake heard Chris stifle a yawn and grinned. "Chris is having a hard time in there. Once Ben starts on something, he certainly gives it a good going over."

"You don't like Chris much, do you?"

"He's OK."

"Why are you so easily threatened?" Laura asked.

"I'm not," said Jake as he saw more keys on a shelf just below the pegs. "Wait a minute – maybe this is it."

"I'm not fussed about the beer."

"I am. I've got a raging thirst."

The key worked and Jake pulled open the cold box impatiently. Then he gave a cry of disgust.

Jake stood there, silently staring down. "I don't believe this," he muttered.

"What is it?" Laura pushed him aside and then began to gag.

In the cold box was a small piece of slime. There was also a faint smell of rotten eggs.

Jake grabbed the intercom to the wheelhouse. "Dad – you'd better get down here. Fast."

"What is it?"

"You should come and see for yourself."

"What's going on?" asked Ben as he came back into the cabin with a tray on which two cups of cocoa steamed. The haze somehow reminded Jake of acid.

"Someone's been collecting slime," he said.

Dan Oakley overheard as he clambered down. "And who the hell would do a thing like that then?"

There was a long silence during which the *Lucky Strike* rocked at anchor, the wind still in her rigging, waves slapping at her bow.

"I just don't get it." Dan was horrified and confused.

They were all four gazing into the cold box now while the sulphurous smell grew more intense. Ben put the tray down carefully on the table with a shaking hand.

"Ben?" asked Dan, turning away from the slime and staring at him curiously. "Do you know anything about this?"

Slowly, reluctantly, his brother nodded.

21

"What *do* you know about it then?" rasped Jake, while everyone else continued to stare at Ben in disbelief. "I thought you said your scientific work didn't include slime."

"Of course it didn't," said Ben shortly.

"Then what *did* the work involve?"

Ben didn't reply and Dan took over the attack. "What were you damned well playing at?"

"I needed the money." Ben's voice had no expression.

"What money?"

"I got into debt down at the pub – had a bit of a flutter on the gee-gees." For some reason Jake was reminded of someone as Ben spoke, but he couldn't think who it was.

"So you grew slime?" asked Chris. "Is that a hobby of yours?"

"I didn't grow it. I was testing the stuff."

"Who for?" Jake was completely bewildered now. His uncle? Testing slime?

"The MOD."

"You mean, you contacted them?"

"They contacted me."

"When?"

"A few weeks ago."

"You knew – and never told us. Even when it all started happening?" Jake was baffled, unable even to begin to believe in what his uncle was saying.

"I didn't know what the stuff was – and when I did, I didn't like to say."

"Why leave the filth on board?" Dan was coldly angry. "It could have killed us all."

"The slime was dead. There *wasn't* any danger. I would have got rid of it but—"

"Why didn't you tell me?" Dan was staring at his brother as if he was a stranger.

Ben looked away. Jake had never seen his father in such a rage.

"Who asked you to test the stuff?"

"Bloke called Harry Baker."

"Why couldn't he test it himself?"

"He didn't say. Maybe he thought he'd look too obvious."

"Did you know him before?"

"I've seen him in the pub."

"I don't get it," said Laura. "Why should someone at Craven Marsh give a local fisherman something as top secret as the slime to test?"

"This man," said Ben slowly, still in a dull monotone, "he wasn't high up at Craven Marsh. I think he was a research assistant in one of the labs. Had a bit of a bee in his bonnet."

"What kind of bee?" asked Dan.

"Baker was scared."

"Why?"

"He said he'd overheard some of the senior staff talking about the experiment running out of control – that there were serious problems and the substance must never be exposed to water for long periods. Baker was being watched, or so he said, and so he asked *me* to expose the stuff."

"And he paid you, out of his own pocket?" Dan sounded incredulous.

"I told you – he was dead scared of what he'd got mixed up in. The stuff needed testing under controlled conditions, but he couldn't handle it himself without being sussed. And he couldn't spill the beans effectively until he knew what *would* happen to the stuff in water – in the sea."

"You must have taken your chance when I was in Chatham," said Dan bitterly.

"As you know, I took the *Strike* out for a day's

fishing. When I was alone I lowered the slime in a lobster pot."

"What happened?" asked Chris with a sudden detached curiosity.

"When I was given the stuff it was the size of a postage stamp. During the few minutes the slime was in the sea it grew to the size you can see in the cold box. I whipped the pot up pretty fast, I can tell you."

Who did Ben remind him of, Jake wondered again. Who was it who always seemed to have a prepared speech, who often seemed to be reading from a carefully prepared script?

"How much were you paid to do this?" asked Laura contemptuously.

"Five hundred quid. Just enough to cover the debt."

"I just don't believe you left it here." Dan had his head in his hands.

"I didn't know what the hell the slime was. Just some kind of chemical."

"But you quickly found out," said Dan bitterly. "You never really cared for me or Jake, did you? always knew you were a main-chancer."

"I never—"

"You could have come to me for the money," Dan continued bitterly. "I could have covered the debt."

"Wait a minute," said Chris. "So the slime grew. Why didn't it grow some more? What did you do

with the stuff after you took it out of the lobster
pot?"

"I left it on deck in the pot for a while and then
the stuff started drying out. So I took it out of the
lobster pot and shoved it in the cold box."

"With your bare hands?"

"No. Harry told me never to touch the stuff. I
used a scoop."

They stared down into the cold box. The piece of
slime was a flaccid grey-green colour, and although
it was slightly shrivelled there were no burnt
patches.

"For God's sake, Ben," began Dan. "You *knew*
about the slime's reaction to water. Why the hell
didn't you tell someone?"

"Correction," Jake realized that Ben was fighting
to keep his credibility, "Craven Marsh knew about
its reaction. It was their responsibility to keep it
under control."

"You've got a funny way of looking at
responsibility," Dan sneered.

"I could have been breaking the Official Secrets
Act," muttered Ben.

"Why didn't you?" Laura accused him. "You
could have saved lives, couldn't you?"

Jake was incredulous. Was this really his Uncle
Ben? The man he had known and loved and relied
on? It didn't seem possible.

"Wait a minute," breathed Laura. "The slime's

not dead. It's pulsating. The cold box must have kept it dormant."

"The slime's been kept cool, in the dark. Maybe that's inhibited growth. But now it's out in the light, however dim—" Ben's voice ground to a halt.

"Get the bloody filthy stuff out of here," yelled Dan.

No one moved.

"Ben – you brought the slime on board. *Do* something." Dan was insistent.

Still Ben didn't move, looking away from them all, his expression sullen.

There's more to this, thought Jake. Much more. But what is it? It was as if they were skating over a frozen lake. All they could see was the icy surface. But what was below the ice? Then he suddenly realized who Ben reminded him of. That prepared explanation. Script-like. Rehearsed. Ben reminded Jake of Andrew Millard.

"I don't think you should throw the slime over board," said Chris. "Not while it's still capable of growing. I think we should leave it in the cold box until the sun comes out tomorrow and then lay it out on the deck. See if the slime shrivels up some more. This can be our own little experiment."

"For God's sake!" Dan was horrified. "You mean we're going to put to sea with a cargo of slime?"

"To meet big brother?" suggested Laura.

"Seems like a good night out," said Ben, trying to return to his usual flip self. He closed the cold-box lid and turned the key in the padlock. "Who wants a nice cup of cocoa before it gets cold?"

"No thanks," said Dan. "We'll never be sure what you put in it."

"The scummy surface on that cold cocoa does look slimy, doesn't it?" commented Jake.

Ben had betrayed them all, but in a way that none of them could understand. All Jake knew was that his uncle had told a pack of lies. But everything that had happened in the last twenty-four hours had been so catastrophic that Ben's strange behaviour almost seemed par for the course.

The *Lucky Strike* chugged away from the shore, showing as few lights as possible. Jake and Dan were in the wheelhouse while Laura, Ben and Chris were out on deck.

Dan was in sombre mood. "How could he have done it?" he kept asking. "Look at the danger Ben's exposed us to."

Jake, however, knew there was more to it than irresponsibility. "There's something else, Dad."

"What?"

He began to explain how he had seen Ben and Andrew Millard together in the Jaguar and how even then his uncle had seemed discomfited.

"And just now," he concluded, "when Ben was

trying to explain himself away, he sounded fake, as if he'd learnt a script – just like Millard."

But Dan had had enough. "What he did was damn stupid, but that's all." He checked the compass. "I don't want to talk about this any more."

They gazed at each other apprehensively as the *Lucky Strike* rounded the point and Ben was put on hold.

There were a few lights far out to sea, but there was no sign of the wallowing slime. The ravaged quayside was lit with arc lights, but only a few soldiers were around and the helicopters were parked on the improvised pad. For an emergency alert, with the slime reaching the harbour, the armed forces and emergency services seemed remarkably unprepared.

Suppose Shingleton was just a test case, thought Jake. Suppose the horrendous nature of the attack on the town was only an exercise to determine the efficacy of the slime? Could the military, the emergency services, the public, all be victims of a government department whose activities were secret – so secret that only a few would know of its existence? If so, how had Ben *really* got mixed up in all this? And what sort of so-called scientific work had he been doing abroad?

"I'll call up Charlie," said Dan, reaching for the radio.

"Isn't that risky?" asked Ben, coming into the

wheelhouse. Jake glanced behind him at Laura and Chris. He was always uneasy when they were alone together.

"We're on the fishing frequency," snapped Dan. "As you know."

"Anyone could be listening in."

Dan sighed. "Maybe you're right. We'll come in behind the stuff. That way we can check the dry dock's open." He seemed to be under increasing strain.

"Charlie may be under orders to keep the gates shut," said Jake. "Why didn't we think of that?"

"He'd find a way round the problem," said Dad with what seemed false certainty.

"Can't the gates be opened from the outside?" asked Jake.

Dan nodded.

"Great," said Ben. "Any volunteers? Please don't count on me."

Then Jake suddenly saw the slime, huge and bulbous, a dark shadow, wallowing in the trough of the waves. "Watch out, Dad."

"I can see it." Dan frowned. "I'm going to try Charlie on the radio."

"You'll blow everything." Ben was scornful.

"I don't think so," he said as he began to dial.

"Harbour Master."

"I'm just off for a spot of night fishing," said Dan cautiously.

"Did you realize that Shingleton's a disaster area?" Charlie's voice was cold and official.

"I still have to earn a living."

"The slime's out there, for God's sake. Get back to your moorings."

"I'm all set up now. I've got fish to catch." Dan sounded truculent.

"Typical of you." There was a little more warmth in Charlie's voice, but Jake was sure that he wasn't alone.

"What's the slime up to?"

"Not a lot."

"So there'll be no more action until morning?"

Charlie Mason didn't reply. "I have to tell you you're taking a serious risk."

"I thought one idea was to try and strand the stuff in the dock."

"Don't be a fool," snapped Charlie. "There's no chance of that. Think of the danger to the town. Think of the death rate we've already got. Do you want it to rise?"

"Of course not. But the sun should be warming up nicely by nine."

There was a long silence, and Jake wondered if Charlie had hung up. Then he began to whisper urgently. "They've been called away."

"Who?"

"Security. I've got a few seconds. I've got problem. The gates *have* stuck. But they've stuck oo soon for our plan."

"You mean, you can't open them? That's the
everse of what we want."

"I've tried, but it's no go. But you know they can
be opened from outside? Can you do it?"

Dan swore.

"It's down to you now, Dan. They're coming
back." Charlie began to speak normally. "I must
warn you that if you try fishing tonight, I'll have you
arrested. Got it?"

"I've got it," said Dan. "I'm going back to
Longshore."

"Let's take another look at the slime's position," said
Ben, to Jake's surprise.

Dan took the *Lucky Strike* in a wider half-circle.
The slime was about fifty metres from the dry dock
whose gates were remote controlled from the
Harbour Master's office. But they could also be
operated from the manual mechanism on the dock
wall.

"Whatever we try to do," said Dan, "is going to be
compromised by any action taken to keep the slime
out of the harbour. In other words, we could be a
target."

"I don't reckon they're going to do anything."
Laura seemed very certain as she turned to Jake.
"Do you?"

He looked out into the dark waves. "That

destroyer's way off." Then he gazed back at the harbour. "And there's no activity on the quayside either."

Dan wasn't so sure. "They could still fire a missile, or shoot us from the harbour wall."

"Honestly, Dad, Charlie said Denver wasn't going to attack the stuff until it was out in the open sea again. Maybe they're actually going to let the thing drift into the harbour, hope it hasn't got enough energy to attack and will drift out again on the tide."

"It depends on who Denver's taking his orders from," Chris observed.

"What's that supposed to mean?" snapped Ben.

Chris didn't reply as the *Lucky Strike* rocked on the swell of the incoming tide.

The slime seemed nearer.

"Let me take the dinghy and try to get those gates open," said Ben suddenly. "I can handle it. I need to make up for that pathetic mistake I made."

One hell of a mistake, thought Jake, wondering yet again what Ben's motives had really been. But there were so many unanswered questions and no time to make connections now.

'If I can get the gates of the dock open," said Ben slowly, "the slime should float straight through the harbour into the dock. Then I'll close them again. That'll leave the slime high and dry."

"What if the army spot what's happening?" asked Laura. "They could open the gates again."

"I've thought of that," grinned Ben. "I'll take that big crowbar with me and jam the mechanism."

"Wait a minute," said Dan. "Let's toss for the job. There's quite a swell and if you capsize—"

"Look, I told you, this is my way of trying to make things up," said Ben. "I did something damn stupid. So I'm going to try and do something damn good. Now, give me a hand lowering that bloody dinghy."

Jake watched his uncle rowing steadily, the dinghy bobbing up and down on the waves, the sea getting rougher as the wind increased. Ben now seemed perilously close to the drifting, wallowing slime and Jake could hardly bear to watch as he stood on the pitching deck.

Then he felt a hand on his arm and turned to see that it was Laura's.

"He's still OK," she said. "The slime's only moving with the tide."

"Do you think it's dead?" asked Jake hopefully.

"I don't think so."

Then Jake saw a tentacle move. "You're right," he said. "It's still alive. For God's sake, Ben, hurry up!" he muttered, his fingernails digging deep into the palms of his hands. Laura's grip on his arm tightened and Jake was aware that Chris was watching them intently.

Ben had almost reached his target when the dinghy was thrown against one of the gates by the swell. He tried to ward himself off with an oar but it broke with a tremendous crack and he was thrown backwards into the stern, capsizing the dinghy.

For a few moments Jake could see nothing but surging waves and he heard his father crying out, calling Ben's name in desperation.

"He's OK," yelled Chris. "He's swimming towards the gates."

"But what about the dinghy?" said Jake. "How the hell's he going to get back?"

"Swim for it?" suggested Laura.

"No way. He'd never be able to fight the tide – and how's he going to jam the wheel? Now the gates can be closed as soon as he's opened them."

"Got an inflatable?" asked Chris.

"In the locker behind the wheelhouse."

"You stay here, Jake," said Laura. "Keep an eye on Ben."

"You'll have to check with Dad," he shouted at her.

"OK," yelled Chris.

Meanwhile, Jake watched Ben drag himself up on to the wall of the dry dock. Then he saw the tentacle moving again, this time more vigorously. The rising swell, the growing smell of sulphur and the slapping waves gave the impression of a dank hell.

Slowly, Ben began to crank at the handle and at first nothing happened. Then, as he tugged harder, the gates of the dry dock slowly began to open and with a roaring, gurgling sound the tide began to pour in. That should wake up the army, Jake thought.

The current eddied against the slime, pushing the thing towards the dock.

But it still had some way to go and Jake knew the opening of the gates could be noticed at any moment.

Then Chris and Laura came back from the wheelhouse to join him.

"We've got the inflatable ready. Laura and I are ready to have a go," yelled Chris, but Laura intervened.

"Your dad said if anyone was to go, it should be you, Jake. You've got the experience."

Jake felt a rush of pride for he knew how much the decision must have cost his father, who would gladly have gone in his place if he'd been fit enough.

"I'll come with you," said Chris.

"OK." Jake was reluctant, but he knew he would need all the help he could get.

"I've found another crowbar," said Laura. "But there's a correction to the running order. If Jake's going, then so am I. Chris, you can get ready to haul us up again."

He began to protest, but Laura told him to shut up.

"We haven't got time to argue." She gazed at Jake. "I'm coming, whatever you say. I'm strong and I'm willing."

Jake knew that to share this with Laura would be highly dangerous, but he also knew he wanted her with him – at all costs.

"We need you here, Chris," said Jake. "It's going to be hell getting into the inflatable in this swell."

Chris turned away. "OK," he said. "Let's get on with it then."

Ben was on the wall now, waving triumphantly, and the slime was drifting lazily, a couple of tentacles flailing, the smell of sulphur slowly increasing.

"Let's pick Ben up," said Jake. "Pay out the line," he told Chris, "and throw the inflatable overboard. We'll take the oars and the crowbar. Then you pull her towards the ladder. Got it?"

"Pull who?" Chris looked a little confused.

"The inflatable, you idiot," said Laura. "Don't you know all boats are female?"

"They would be," he replied in a hollow voice, pitching the inflatable into the waves.

"I'll go first," said Jake to Laura. "I'll take the oars and you take the crowbar." He scrambled over the side of the *Lucky Strike* and on to the ladder, while Laura followed shakily, clutching the heavy crowbar.

She got down the ladder but then tripped, falling into the inflatable with a heavy thud, almost overturning the frail little craft.

"You OK?" shouted Jake.

"Sort of."

"What did you say about all boats being female?" shouted Chris, but neither Jake nor Laura heard him.

"Stow that crowbar under your seat and I'll row towards Ben," gasped Jake.

"Where do I sit?"

"In the stern. At the back," he yelled. "Get there fast or we'll capsize!"

"Maybe Chris should have gone with you," she muttered weakly.

"I don't want Chris," yelled Jake. "I only want you. That's all I've ever wanted. Don't you understand?"

"I understood that a long time ago."

Her remark made him uneasy, but he had no time to worry about what she meant.

Jake took a quick glance at the slime. He could see the blue veins, the blunt head, the moving tentacles, and there was definitely a slight haze of acid in the moonlight as the sea slapped at its flabby bulk.

Jake rowed from the *Lucky Strike* towards the dry

dock in the bumpy current, drawing nearer to Ben, while Laura craned her neck to keep the slime in sight.

The stuff seemed to be bearing down on them much faster now.

"Row harder!"

"I can't." But as he spoke the inflatable was bumping up against the wall of the dry dock. "We've got another crowbar," Jake shouted to Ben.

"Chuck it to me!"

Laura scrabbled under her seat, finally dragging it out and lobbing the crowbar at Ben as hard as she could.

"OK," he yelled, "I've got it."

"Move!" yelled Jake. "The slime's on its way."

But Ben seemed to be taking a very long time ramming the crowbar into the mechanism, and even when he appeared to have succeeded he still remained, crouching there.

"For God's sake—" yelled Jake.

The slime was even nearer now.

Then Jake heard a shout from above and looking up saw a soldier standing on the quayside, pointing a rifle at them.

"Get away!" he shouted.

"We can't," shouted back Laura, improvising hurriedly. "The slime attacked our trawler."

"I can't hear you," shouted the soldier.

Finally Ben straightened up and then jumped,

landing awkwardly in the inflatable between Jake and Laura, and making the rubber craft sink even lower in the water.

Jake glanced desperately behind him, only to see the slime was within a few metres of them.

"Row," shouted Ben. "Row like hell!"

"I am!"

"You're not. Go faster – or I'll take over."

"What the hell are you doing?" yelled the soldier, his rifle still raised. He obviously wasn't sure whether to shoot or not. Jake could see other figures running along the wrecked quayside and knew they weren't going to be fooled for long. So they could be shot or they could be decimated by the slime. What the hell was the difference anyway?

The slime was towering above them now, heaving on the swell, slowly turning, acidic steam rising. Jake felt numb as he rowed on, ducking as a tentacle flailed above him.

Looking back, Jake saw to his horror that the *Lucky Strike* was also slowly chugging into the harbour towards them.

"Get back, Dad," he shouted. "Get back." But Jake knew neither Chris nor his father stood a chance of hearing him.

The slime was now wallowing between the trawler and the inflatable, tentacles flailing, the smell of sulphur overpowering. The moon shone down steadily, bathing the deadly mass in a halo of light, the blunted head turning towards the trawler.

"The slime's going for them," screamed Laura.

"What in God's name is Dan doing?" shouted Ben. "Why doesn't he back off?"

Because he's trying to rescue us, thought Jake. That's what he's trying to do – and the slime's going to kill him. The tears stung his eyes. He had no one in the world except for his dad – and Ben.

The tentacles lashed out again, this time hitting a wave in a cloud of phosphorous acidic steam, landing within a couple of metres of the *Lucky Strike*. Then they lashed again and suddenly hit her prow, the acid melting metal and wood, holing her immediately.

"Jump!" yelled Jake. A sheet of flame flared in the night.

Jake was rowing alongside the slime, gasping for breath, his muscles screaming, clenching his teeth. He rowed on, only thinking about Dad and Chris, putting everything into pitting his strength against the slime and sea. He hadn't the slightest fear for himself or his passengers.

Then he turned, glancing over his shoulder, and saw that the *Lucky Strike* had disappeared into what looked like a black hole in the waves.

"Dan," stammered Ben. "It's taken Dan."

Laura was silent, her head bowed, hands over her

eyes, while the slime drifted in the waves beside them, huge and monolithic.

Jake began to row furiously again, finally distancing them from the slime as the tide took it through the jammed-open dock gates. There were shouts from the quayside, shots cracked out but Jake knew there was nothing they could do.

He heard a snapping sound which he reckoned was the crowbar finally breaking in two under incredible pressure. Then the gates began to close, the mechanism spinning uselessly. But Jake could see the slime was trapped inside the dock and he felt a heady rush of triumph that immediately evaporated when he thought of the fate of the *Lucky Strike* and the death of the most important person in his life.

When Jake arrived at the spot where the trawler had gone down, he put down the oars and wept. "Dad," he whispered. "Oh – Dad."

Ben put an arm round his shoulders. "I'll look out for you," he said inadequately. Then he turned to Laura. "I'm sorry," he said. "Terribly sorry about Chris. I don't know what to say."

She didn't reply, but slowly Laura reached out a hand to Jake.

23

When the shouting began Jake couldn't at first make out where it was coming from. Then, in disbelief, he recognized a familiar voice.

"Dad?" he bellowed. "Is it really you?"

"Chris?" yelled Laura.

"We're over here!" Dan Oakley sounded weak but determined. "I've got Chris."

"Keep talking to us," called Jake as he rowed towards their voices, finally spotting the dark figures in the water, hanging on to a couple of life-belts.

Somehow they dragged Dan and Chris over the side of the inflatable and the little craft sank even lower. Meanwhile, sirens wailed in the harbour and more lights came on.

"If they find out what we've done," said Laura, "we're going to be in big trouble."

"You can say that again. I mean – all we've done is rescue the world from the slime monster from Craven Marsh. Isn't that enough? After all, they didn't exactly help, did they? And we still don't know why."

Jake strained once again at the oars, heading towards the beach beyond the harbour, battling against the tide.

"Let me take over," said Ben. "You're not getting anywhere." Somehow they managed to shift positions and he began to row strongly, bumping through the waves, sheets of spray breaking over them.

Jake and Laura lay on the beach, drained, shivering violently. The others were a few metres away, totally exhausted.

Sirens still resounded in the harbour and there was a flurry of activity with vehicles moving and a couple of helicopters buzzing ineffectively over the slime in the dry dock.

"I wonder what they thought about the delivery we made." Jake suddenly laughed. He couldn't believe they were all safe.

"I'm sorry about the *Lucky Strike*," said Laura.

Jake sat up, hugging his knees. There was a long pause. Then he said, "Is there a chance then?"

"What for?"

"You and me?"

"I was hoping you wouldn't ask that."

"Am I at least in with a chance?"

"A chance is *all* you've got—"

Jake knew that he would have to be satisfied with that, at least for the moment.

Dan stiffly clambered to his feet. "We'll catch our deaths out here," he said. "We need to get moving."

"Where?" asked Jake.

"Remember Paddy's old shed up the beach? It's not far from here."

"Who's Paddy?" asked Laura.

"He's a retired fisherman," said Jake. "If he lived in the town he'd just fold up and die – slime, or no slime. Right now, he sounds like a soul-mate."

After half an hour's long and painful walk, stiff, sore, bedraggled and still soaking wet, the shivering group arrived at a tin shack on the beach-head.

A grey dawn was slowly breaking and the wind had dropped, the waves crawling over the pebbles, making a grating sound.

Dan Oakley knocked at the door of the shed, breaking the early morning silence.

After what seemed a very long time an old man

opened the door, gnarled, leathery and thin as a stick.

"Paddy," said Dan, "can you give us a bit of shelter?"

"I can for you." His voice was a husky whisper. "But you'll have to fend for yourself. I haven't got the strength."

The interior of the shack was filthy, piled with bundles of newspapers, cast-off clothing, opened tins and unwashed dishes.

"Do you want to hear what's been happening?" asked Dan while Ben, Jake, Laura and Chris hovered nervously by the door, feeling claustrophobic.

"No, I don't," snapped Paddy. "I don't want to know what's going on in the world. I've had enough of that. So whatever's happened, whatever trouble you're in, whatever state the world's in – even if it's Armageddon, I don't want to know." Paddy turned towards the door. "I don't want to be inhospitable, but I always watch the sunrise, whatever the weather. I don't much like being indoors, and if I have my way I'll die out there. Dan – why don't you boil the kettle and there's some biscuits in that tin on the shelf. I reckon there's going to be a sunrise this morning that's worth seeing."

Any sunrise would be worth seeing, thought Jake.

* * *

Chris, Laura and Jake sat against a breakwater, drinking hot, strong tea from ancient mugs and gorging themselves on shortbread biscuits. Never had they been so hungry and thirsty. Never had they had such a wonderful feast.

The three men sat further up the beach, their talk a comforting background drone.

All's well, thought Jake, gazing up at the red orb of a sun rising out of a bank of mist, I'm sure it is.

The sun rose slowly over a calm sea, the pale blue sky cloudless and holding a promise of heat.

"I'm sorry," said Jake to Chris. "I've acted like a spoilt kid."

"We've all been stupid," Chris replied. "That's what fear does to you. It strips away the years."

"Like the slime could have stripped away the world," said Laura, taking a last sip of her tea.

"It could still do that." Jake looked up the beach towards Shingleton.

"What do you mean?" She was wide awake now and fearful. So was Chris, and Jake wished he hadn't spoken. It was so peaceful, so hopeful here. Why did he have to spoil it all?

"I just hope the sun's going to do the trick. We need roast slime. Nothing less will do."

"It's *going* to be hot," said Chris, looking up at the deepening blue of the sky.

"I hope so." Jake felt compelled to voice his anxiety.

"What's the matter?" asked Laura.

"The slime had had time to get its strength back in the sea. Maybe it got out of the dock. Maybe it's creating havoc in the town again."

"We can soon find out," said Laura, but her eyes were closing again. Jake felt a heavy weight pressing down on his own lids, and when he glanced across at Chris, he saw that he was lying on his back, snoring.

Jake tried to stop himself from lying down on the pebbles. He *had* to sit up. He *had* to keep awake.

Then the merciful, healing sleep suddenly swept him with all the force of an incoming tide.

Jake woke sweating, lying in a blaze of hot sunshine. But it wasn't the heat that woke him for he was sure he had heard the most primitive, the most agonizing howling sound, like a huge animal in the most excruciating pain.

He sat up, head pounding, shivering again despite the heat, and looked back. His father and uncle and Paddy were staring down the beach towards Shingleton, and putting their hands to their ears as the howling got louder and more excruciating.

Jake staggered to his feet, the noise getting into his eardrums, making them ache with pain. Then, he, too, clapped his hands over his ears, reeling and giddy and crying out with the agony of it all.

Then he saw Chris and Laura were standing by the edge of the sea, the waves splashing their feet.

What were they staring at so intently?

As Jake watched them suspiciously, the howling lessened and rattled away to nothing at all.

There was a long, long silence.

Laura and Chris still stood by the edge of the sea, staring out as intently as before.

What were they doing? Together?

"The slime's dead," said his father slowly.

Jake turned and stared back at the three men who were shimmering in the heat haze.

In his sleep, he had kicked off his shoes and the pebbles were hard and hot. "What?" he yelled. "What did you say?"

"The slime's dead," his father repeated.

"How do you know?"

"That was a death rattle, wasn't it?"

Jake still wasn't sure.

He plunged over the boiling hot pebbles, wondering why Laura and Chris still hadn't turned round.

What could they be staring at?

When he arrived at the edge of the sea, Jake saw that Chris and Laura were standing slightly apart, staring out at the waves that were steely and shimmering in the increasing heat.

Then he saw it too.

24

Something was making slow but steady progress past the beach. It was grey-green.

"What is it?" whispered Jake.

"I don't know," said Chris. His face was expressionless.

"I don't think it's anything to worry about." Laura's voice was flat.

"I'll tell Dad." Jake began to run back up the beach towards his father, oblivious to the burning pain in his feet. When he reached him, he gasped out, "There's something out there. It's floating up the coast."

"The slime's dead," said Dan with complete assurance and Ben nodded in agreement.

"I'm going back inside for my morning nap."

Paddy turned back to the door of his shack. "I don't want to hear this."

"Neither do I," said Ben.

"That's been the trouble all along." Jake was desperate. "No one wants to listen."

"Don't get paranoid, son." His father was irritated now.

"Come and see."

"What's the point?"

Why was Dad being so blockish, wondered Jake.

"*Please* come and see, Dad." Jake felt a child again, urging on a reluctant parent to play a game.

Father and son scrunched over the pebbles together, but Jake had never felt so alone.

"It's gone," said Chris, once they were back at the edge of the sea.

Jake gazed up the coast. "Look, it's shining in the sun." But he could only see a silvery flash which could have been anything. Was he *sure* he'd seen a piece of slime. Could it have been something else? Seawrack? Plankton? Plastic?

"We were just imagining things." Laura glanced up at Chris and he put his arm round her.

It was as if they had both formed a conspiracy against him. They could have seen anything. So could he. Maybe there'd been no slime at all. Jake felt safer as he began to betray himself.

His father was silent, staring out to sea.

"I must have been mistaken, Dad."

"Maybe you were, son."

An hour later, Jake, Dan, Ben, Chris and Laura joined the jostling crowds on what was left of the harbour wall, looking down at the dried-out slime. It had spread over the mud of the dry dock, a grey carcass from which flies rose, gulls hovering over the dead flesh.

An early edition of the *Mail* fluttered on a bench and Jake picked the paper up, amazed that the headlines made no mention of Shingleton.

"This is so weird," he said aloud.

"What is?"

"Hundreds dead, the town in ruins and not a word in the paper."

Jake went on leafing through the *Mail* until he came to a small news item at the bottom of page six, just before the international news:

KENT CHEMICAL LEAK

A chemical leak which spread up the Kent coast to Shingleton from the Craven Marsh MOD research station has been cleared by police and an army division from Folkestone. An investigation is being carried out, but a spokesman for Craven Marsh has been reported as stating: "There was some minimal damage to property, but the situation is now contained."

Jake passed the paper to Laura who read it through in disgust. "They've done a total cover-up," she said. "How?"

"Who are 'they'?" he asked.

Ben picked up the paper. "We've all got too much to lose."

"What do you mean – lose?" demanded Chris.

"Well – we want the insurance on the *Lucky Strike*. People need to rebuild, to be compensated, to replace vehicles, renew the infrastructure. I mean – Shingleton will need a new leisure centre now."

"That's just bribery," snarled Jake. "You won't allow a cover-up, will you, Dad?"

But Dan had no chance to reply as Chris and Laura both spotted their parents standing on the opposite side of the harbour.

"Thank God," said Laura, overwhelmed with joy, and Chris gave her a quick peck on the cheek.

"Wait a minute," Jake yelled at them. "What about this cover-up?"

"We'll talk about it later," she said and then they both disappeared into the crowd. To Jake, it was as if they had disappeared for ever.

Once again he felt a devastating sense of isolation.

Then Jake saw Millard walking towards them. He looked as he had a couple of days ago – days that now seemed light years away. He was wearing his blazer, a white shirt, old school tie and neatly pressed trousers and a pair of black shoes. He looked out of place in the devastated surroundings, but completely in control.

"Hello, Jake," said Millard quietly, nodding at Ben and Dan. "I hear you've turned out quite the hero."

"How did you hear that?"

"I've got my sources." He pulled out an envelope from the inside pocket of his blazer. "Strictly speaking I should be giving this to your dad, but since you've been so – resourceful – I thought I'd officially hand it over to you."

"What is it?" But Jake knew what it was.

"A cheque that I think you'll find will more than cover the cost of a new trawler with quite a bit left over."

"Like my bike," said Jake bitterly.

"Exactly like your bike." Millard smiled appreciatively, his smile extending to Dan and Ben.

"You'll be compensating thousands."

"Exactly," said Millard. "That's the least we can do."

"And the dead?"

"Their families will be cared for."

"And the damage?"

"Everything will be rebuilt."

"With a quite bit left over for everyone?"

"Exactly," Millard repeated. The smile never left his face.

"And the press?"

"That's a government decision."

Then Jake decided to voice his suspicion – the terrible suspicion that he knew would hurt his father so much – but he couldn't keep quiet any longer. He had to be sure. "What about my Uncle Ben?"

"What about him?" Millard's smile froze on his lips.

"Does he work for you?"

"I don't understand."

Jake glanced at Ben who gazed steadily back at him. There was no expression on his face at all.

"Jake!" Dan shouted. "What the hell are you saying? How dare you—"

"Here's your cheque." Jake passed his father the envelope. "That should shut you up."

Ben suddenly and surprisingly intervened. "Andrew, I think Jake has a right to know."

Millard sighed. "I'd hoped it wouldn't come to this." He paused. Then he said slowly, "I'm going to confide in you, but if I hear that the information has been passed to *anyone*, you'll be arrested immediately." He paused again. "For some years, your uncle has been helping us professionally at Craven Marsh."

"In what capacity?" Dan sounded as if he couldn't believe this, didn't want to believe this.

"A consultant, largely working abroad."

"What does that mean exactly?" asked Jake belligerently.

"It means he's been making some assessments for us."

"That's a meaningless statement."

Millard held his gaze. "Let's put it another way. Your uncle is working in the national interest."

Jake turned to Ben. "How exactly *is* this in the national interest?"

"I'm afraid I can't say," he replied.

"Was the slime a weapon that went wrong, or a weapon you needed to test?"

"You're big on fantasy, aren't you, Jake?" Millard seemed amused.

"I'm talking to Ben," snarled Jake.

"As I said before, I'm afraid I can't comment."

"I know your father won't discuss this," said Millard, "but if *you* do, Jake, there'll be ramifications I'm afraid."

"What kind of ramifications?"

"A withdrawal of compensation for a start. Your dad needs a living and so will you. Eventually."

Jake felt an even stronger sense of isolation. Dad had been bribed, Chris and Laura already seemed to be putting it all behind them. Jake was on his own, and, just like his father, he too had been given a cheque.

He gazed down at the rotting, fly-blown carcass of the slime. "You won't always get away with this," he said to Millard. But he also meant it for Ben.

"The crowds are going to be cleared," said his

uncle, giving Jake a warm and friendly smile – a smile that seemed to echo Millard's. "The town will be evacuated and closed. The dead will be buried."

"I'll call the press," said Jake. "I don't care what happens to me."

"Who would listen to a kid?" asked Ben quietly.